SPECIAL MESSAGE TO READERS

This book is published under the auspices of
THE ULVERSCROFT FOUNDATION
(registered charity No. 264873 UK)

Established in 1972 to provide funds for
research, diagnosis and treatment of eye diseases.
Examples of contributions made are: —

A new Children's Assessment Unit at
Moorfield's Hospital, London.

•

Twin operating theatres at the
Western Ophthalmic Hospital, London.

•

A Chair of Ophthalmology at the
University of Leicester.

•

The establishment of a Royal Australian College
of Ophthalmologists "Fellowship".

You can help further the work of the Foundation
by making a donation or leaving a legacy. Every
contribution, no matter how small, is received
with gratitude. Please write for details to:

**THE ULVERSCROFT FOUNDATION,
The Green, Bradgate Road, Anstey,
Leicester LE7 7FU, England.
Telephone: (0116) 236 4325**

**In Australia write to:
THE ULVERSCROFT FOUNDATION,
c/o The Royal Australian College of
Ophthalmologists,
27, Commonwealth Street, Sydney,
N.S.W. 2010.**

VALLEY OF FEAR

Jason Ballard, owner of the Circle B spread, was set on forcing the homesteaders out of the valley. But just as he mounted an operation to intimidate the settlers, Dan Kilcane, an ex-cavalry lieutenant, rode in and upset the rancher's plans. But when the rancher brings in the Liquidators, a notorious quartet of professional gunslingers, will Dan and his allies be able to continue thwarting Ballard's plans? Judge Colt would decide.

Books by Alan Irwin
in the Linford Western Library:

BODIE
THE TROUBLE HUNTER
THE LONG TRAIL
BRANAGAN'S LAW

ALAN IRWIN

VALLEY
OF FEAR

Complete and Unabridged

LINFORD
Leicester

First published in Great Britain in 1996 by
Robert Hale Limited
London

First Linford Edition
published 1997
by arrangement with
Robert Hale Limited
London

British Library CIP Data

Irwin, Alan *1916*–
   Valley of fear.—Large print ed.—
   Linford western library
   1. Western stories
   2. Large type books
   I. Title
   823.9′14 [F]

   ISBN 0–7089–5140–6

Published by
F. A. Thorpe (Publishing) Ltd.
Anstey, Leicestershire

Set by Words & Graphics Ltd.
Anstey, Leicestershire
Printed and bound in Great Britain by
T. J. International Ltd., Padstow, Cornwall

This book is printed on acid-free paper

1

AS Dan Kilcane rode down from the high ground, on a clear spring day, he had a panoramic view of the valley below. Looking ahead, then from left to right, across the broad expanse of the valley, he could see that it was first-rate cattle country, well-stocked with grazing cows.

In the distance, he could see dimly, through the haze, some homesteads lined up along the right bank of the river, tree-fringed here and there, which snaked along the valley floor.

Riding in a north-westerly direction, Dan had crossed the Nebraska/Wyoming border three days before, following the North Platte River, and had spent a night at Fort Laramie, before continuing his ride. He had no fixed destination. He had never been to Wyoming before, and for some time he had had a hankering to look the Territory over.

Two and a half days after leaving Fort Laramie, and heading almost due north, he had come across the valley into which he was now riding. It ran roughly northward in front of him. He headed for the homesteads, and as he drew closer to them, he could see how well-situated the quarter sections were, with the river forming their western boundaries. Rangeland, with grazing cows, came right down to the west bank of the river.

As Dan reached the nearest homestead, he swung off the trail, which ran along the valley, east of the river, and headed for the homestead buildings, intending to ask for directions to the nearest town. He could see a house, a large barn, and some sheds. As he drew closer, he saw a woman standing outside the door of the house. Close to her, two men stood facing her, holding the reins of their horses.

The woman was around thirty, slim, with auburn hair. The two men were

2

dressed like cowhands. Each of them was carrying a six-gun, in a right-hand holster, and each of them looked like he knew how to use it. As Dan came to a stop near them, they both turned, and gave him a long, hard look. They saw a well-built man in his early thirties, fair-haired, deeply-tanned, and around five ten. He was wearing clothing of good quality, including a smart black Montana Peak hat. They paid special attention to the long-barrelled Colt .45 Peacemaker in the holster resting against Dan's right hip.

Dan waited a moment, but neither the men nor the woman spoke. He touched his hat, and spoke to the woman.

"Howdy, ma'am," he said. "Just called in for some directions. I'm a stranger, passing through."

Ignoring Dan, the two men mounted their horses. The taller of the two spoke to the woman.

"Remember what I told you," he

said harshly, then rode off with his companion.

The woman looked after them. There was a look of desperation on her face, and she was close to tears. She bowed her head for a moment, then lifted it, and turned to Dan.

"I'm sorry," she said. "How can I help you?"

"Well, ma'am," said Dan. "I'd be obliged if you'd tell me which way I head to get to the nearest town."

"That's Lorimer," she said. "Five miles further down the valley. Just follow the river. You'll see the town from the trail pretty soon."

"I'm obliged, ma'am," said Dan. "It's plain to see," he went on, "that you're mighty worried about something. Anything I can do to help?"

She turned away from him, and bowed her head again. Dan could see her shoulders heaving, as she sobbed uncontrollably. He dismounted, and stood, awkwardly, as she gradually brought herself under control. She turned to face him again.

"No," she replied. "The fix we're in, I'm sure you couldn't do anything about. You'd be up against Jason Ballard, of the Circle B. Those two men who just left, were his foreman Boyle, he's the tall one, and Frazer, one of his hands."

"This Ballard ranches in the valley?" asked Dan.

"He's the *only* rancher in the valley," she replied.

"And he don't like settlers?" asked Dan.

"He hates them," she replied, "but what bothers me most just now, is my husband. He took ill about a week ago, soon after he got back from Casper, where he'd been visiting his parents. He's been laid up ever since. He's real bad, and he ain't getting any better. He's lost all his strength. I just don't know what to do to help him."

"What does the doctor say?" asked Dan.

"That's the trouble," she replied.

"There's a doctor in Lorimer called Harper, but I can't get him out here. Three times, I've sent word to him that John's pretty bad, and asked him to come out right away, but he's never showed up."

"Right," said Dan. "There's one thing I can do then. I'll ride into Lorimer, and bring the doctor back myself."

"It won't be as easy as that," she said. "I don't know who told him, but Ballard knows that John's sick. His men told me, just before you turned up, that Ballard wanted to pay us to transfer our quarter section over to him, and as soon as we did this, he'd see that the doctor came out right away. They're coming back for our answer early tomorrow. I'm going in to my husband John now, to tell him what they said. Our name's Rennie, by the way."

"Kilcane, Dan Kilcane," said Dan. "Before I head for Lorimer, maybe I could see your husband?"

She looked at him, doubtfully.

"You're still figuring to go for the doctor, then?" she said.

He nodded.

"Come inside," she said, and Dan followed her, through to the small bedroom at the back. Rennie was lying on his back on the bed, his head and shoulders propped up with pillows. He didn't look so good, thought Dan. His eyes opened as they came in.

Martha Rennie introduced Dan to him, and told her husband of Dan's intention to go for the doctor. She also told him about the visit of Ballard's men. As she was speaking, Dan took a good look at the homesteader. He showed all the signs of having a fever, and he seemed to be having trouble with his breathing. He nodded weakly at Dan, when his wife had finished speaking. "How d'you feel now, John?" his wife asked him.

"Not so good," he replied, hoarsely. "This fever's burning me up, and that sore throat I told you about ain't

7

getting no better. Feels like it's closing up. And I feel as weak as a baby."

He spoke to Dan.

"I've got to warn you," he said. "If you manage to get a doctor out here, Ballard ain't going to like it."

"That's all right," said Dan. "I'd better be on my way."

He left the bedroom with Rennie's wife, and spoke to her outside the house, before he mounted his horse.

"I've got an idea about what may be ailing your husband," he said, "but only because I've seen something like it before, when I was in a town in West Kansas. There was an epidemic of diphtheria there, and I looked after a friend of mine who was hit. We need to get a doctor here as quick as we can.

"It's a mighty infectious illness," he went on, "so you'd better cover your mouth and nose when tending to your husband, so you don't breathe any germs in. Leastways, that's what I did. I'll be back as soon as I can."

As Dan approached Lorimer, he

could see it was a fair-sized town, built near the west bank of the river. On the north side of town, the homesteads continued along the east bank of the river. There was a fording place opposite the town. He crossed the river at this point, and rode along the main street, until he spotted a 'DOCTOR' sign projecting from the upper floor of a two-storey building standing next to the bank. Steps up the side wall of the building led to a door with a doctor's shingle on it. Dan dismounted, climbed the steps, and knocked on the door.

It was opened by a small, neatly-dressed man, in his fifties, with grey hair and moustache.

"My name's Kilcane," said Dan. "I've just come from the homestead of a man called Rennie. He needs you bad. I reckon that maybe he's got diphtheria. He took ill soon after he got back from a visit to Casper."

"You a friend of Rennie's?" asked Harper.

"No," replied Dan. "I just happened to call in at his place this morning, when two Circle B men were leaving. Mrs Rennie told me that she'd sent word three times, with neighbours, for you to come out to her husband, but it seems the Circle B men said that there was no chance of you showing up at the homestead until Rennie had agreed to transfer his quarter section to Ballard."

"So that's what it's all about," said Harper. "Ballard must've heard about Rennie being ill, and figured it was the right time to pressure him to sell. What happened was that I got Mrs Rennie's messages, and set off for the homestead three times, but three times I was turned round, and escorted back to town by Ballard's men. They just said that Rennie didn't need a doctor.

"And now," he went on, "Ballard's put a man in here with me, to make sure I don't leave to go to Rennie's place. He's a man called Tracy. He told me he's going to stay here all night, and as long after that as Ballard tells him to. Just before you got here, he went to the restaurant across the street there, for a meal. Said he'd be back when he'd finished. But he's sitting against a window, and he can see my door, so there ain't no chance of me leaving without him knowing. And he told me to light that lamp at the top of the stairs, as soon as it was getting dark, which it is now."

He excused himself, and went out to light the lamp. Then, at his request, Dan described the symptoms of Rennie's illness.

"I think maybe you're right," said Harper, when Dan had finished. "It sure sounds like diphtheria. And I heard yesterday that there's been an epidemic in Casper, with a lot of deaths. I've got to see Rennie right away. I saw a few cases of diphtheria before I came here, and I've got a few ideas that might help him. Ballard ain't got no right to stop me from seeing Rennie. I'm going to try again."

11

"Just a minute," said Dan. "I'm going to put Tracy out of action. Then I'm going to ride with you, back to the Rennie homestead."

"You sure you know what you're getting into?" asked the doctor. "Ballard is a powerful and dangerous man."

"And a man who needs teaching a lesson, by the look of it," said Dan. "Ain't there any law around here?"

"We've got a county sheriff called Brand, with an office in town," replied Harper, "but it ain't no use me going to him. Ballard had a big hand in getting him appointed, and he won't do anything Ballard don't like.

"But tell me," he went on, "what your plan is for getting rid of Tracy."

"*You* get ready to leave," said Dan. "I'm going down to the restaurant, and when Tracy leaves to come back here, I'll deal with him. I'll tie him, and gag and blindfold him, then I'll come up here for you. Where can we hide him away till morning?"

"Dave Arnold, who owns the livery

stable next door, is a good friend of mine," said Harper, "and he's one of the few around here who ain't scared of Ballard. Maybe we can leave him at the back of the livery stable. I'll ask Dave. I have to go there for my horse, when you've taken care of Tracy."

Dan left, and walked over to the restaurant. Harper had given him a brief description of Tracy, and he spotted the Circle B man, seated at a window, almost immediately. He was a small man, alert-looking, with sandy hair. Dan asked for a coffee, and sat down.

A quarter of an hour later, Tracy called for his bill. Dan, who had already paid, got up, and walked out. He looked up and down the street. It was deserted. He walked up to the bottom of the steps leading to the doctor's residence, and slipping behind them, he waited in the deep shadow cast by the stairway. A few minutes later, Tracy came out of the restaurant, and headed for the steps. As he started to climb them, Dan slipped out, came up behind him, and struck him on the back of his head with the long barrel of his Peacemaker.

As Tracy slumped, Dan caught him, and dragged him round to the back of the building, where he had left his horse. He tied, gagged and blindfolded Tracy, left him lying in the shadow, then went up the stairs, and returned a few moments later with Harper, who was carrying his bag.

Dan slung Tracy over his shoulder, and carried him to the back of the livery stable. Harper followed in silence, leading Dan's horse and walked into the stable. Soon after, he emerged with Arnold, the owner, and his own horse. Without speaking, he beckoned to Dan to follow him to the far corner of a small corral behind the stable, where Dan dumped Tracy on the ground, and ran a rope from his feet to a fence post. The Circle B man was just starting to regain consciousness as Dan and Harper left to rejoin Arnold, waiting outside the stable.

"Nobody'll see him till morning," said Harper, "by which time I figure I'll be back home. Hope this don't cause you any trouble, Dave."

"Don't see why it should," said Arnold. "Anybody could've dumped him there. Just after daylight, I'll make out I found him in the corral myself, and cut him loose."

Dan and Harper left, and rode to the Rennie homestead. Relief showed in Martha Rennie's face, as she let them into the house.

"He's getting worse," she said. "His breathing ain't good at all. I sure am glad to see you, doctor."

They went through to the bedroom, and Harper examined Rennie thoroughly.

"You were right," he said to Dan. "I can tell from looking at his throat. But I figure I can help him. Just leave him to me and Martha for a while."

Dan went through to the living-room, and waited. After half an hour, the doctor and Martha Rennie came out of the bedroom.

"I reckon he'll be all right," said Harper. "I just got here in time. He's a fit man, and I've got him breathing easier. But he'll have to stay in bed and rest, for two or three weeks. I'll leave plenty of medicine with you. He's lucky. It's a disease we don't have much idea of how to fight, and it kills maybe one in three of the ones who catch it.

"I've had a good look at Martha," he went on, "and it looks like she ain't caught the infection up to now.

"I'd better explain to you, Mr Kilcane," he continued, "that Ballard's a newcomer here. The previous owner of the Circle B, a widower called Barrett, died about three months ago. He got on fine with the homesteaders. In fact, he helped them out in a lot of small ways. But all his kin were in the East, and none of them wanted to take over a cattle ranch. So Ballard bought the spread, and it was a bad day for the settlers in the valley when that happened.

"He'd hardly settled in," continued Harper, "when he started to intimidate the settlers. It's plain that he wants all the range in the valley for himself, so he can build up his herd. He just ignores the fact that the homesteaders have a legal right to their quarter sections. I guess he figures that if he can scare a few of the homesteaders enough, so that they move out, the rest will soon follow."

Dan spoke to Martha Rennie.

"And how do you feel about the situation, Mrs Rennie?" he asked.

"A lot better now I know John will likely get well again," she replied. "We're both set on staying here. We like farming in this valley. And we don't see why Ballard should be allowed to run us off."

The doctor got up to leave.

"You coming to town with me?" he asked Dan.

Dan shook his head.

"If Mr and Mrs Rennie want me to," he said, "I'll stay on here to help out with the work till he's fit again. And I'd like to be here when Ballard's men call for their answer in the morning, just in case they try to make trouble."

Martha Rennie stared at Dan. She heaved a great sigh of relief.

"I've got to admit," she said, "I've been worried sick over what might happen when those men come back. But I can't see why you're offering to stay on and help us, and maybe get yourself hurt."

"It's like this," explained Dan. "It always sticks in my craw, when I hear of somebody like Ballard riding roughshod over people who just ain't able to fight back. There's something inside me tells me I've got to try and do something about it. I try and reason with myself, and tell myself what a fool I am, but it ain't no use."

"We're both very grateful," she said. "You can bed down in the barn."

Dan turned to Harper.

"You should be back in Lorimer well before daylight," he said. "Nobody there but Arnold will know you've been out here, and nobody'll be able to prove you had anything to do with Tracy being pistol-whipped."

"I'll leave, then," said Harper. "I'm pretty sure John's on the mend now, Martha, but get word to me if he don't keep on improving."

After supper, Dan talked for a while with Martha Rennie. She told him what a contented, settled community it had been before rancher Jed Barrett of the Circle B had died, and how things had changed for the worse when Ballard took over. It was quite common nowadays, she said, for the Circle B hands to shout threats and insults at the settlers when the hands rode past the homesteads, or met the settlers in town. And some of the homesteaders were getting scared.

When she broke off, to see to her husband, Dan left, to bed down in the barn.

19

2

DAN woke early the next morning, washed outside, and then went in for breakfast. Martha Rennie had it ready for him, and he sat down to eat.

"How's Mr Rennie doing?" he asked.

"His fever's down a bit," she replied, "and his throat ain't so bad. I think he's past the worst."

"That's good news," said Dan. "Maybe I can see him after breakfast, to find out what jobs he'd like me to do."

"All right," she said. "I know there's plenty of work waiting to be done. We're mighty grateful for your help."

When Dan saw Rennie after breakfast, the homesteader told him about several jobs that needed doing.

"You done any farming before?" he asked Dan.

"I ran my father's homestead near

Ogallala for a spell, after he died," replied Dan.

Some time later, he was splitting some logs outside the house, when he spotted two riders, about half a mile away, approaching the homestead. He went into the barn for his gunbelt, and buckled it on. Then he called Mrs Rennie out, and they watched together, as the riders drew closer.

"Looks like the Circle B men who were here yesterday," said Dan.

She nodded. "That's Boyle and Frazer all right," she said.

The riders stopped in front of them, a few yards away. Boyle, the foreman, was a stocky, surly-looking man. His companion Frazer, was thin and tallish, with a straggly moustache. Remembering Dan from the previous day, they looked surprised to see him still there. Boyle scowled at Dan, then spoke to Martha Rennie.

"We've come for your answer to that proposition we put to you yesterday," he said.

"We're not selling," she said. "We're staying here. This is our land, and Ballard can threaten us as much as he likes, but we're not quitting."

"Mr Ballard don't deal with women," said Boyle, harshly. "We'll go inside, and see your husband. Maybe we can make him see sense."

The two prepared to dismount.

"Hold it!" said Dan. "The lady's given you your answer. You're not going in the house. You're going to turn round, and ride off this homestead. The lady's told me you ain't welcome here. You're trespassing."

The two men stared down at Dan. He was standing, shoulders just slightly hunched, his right hand close to the handle of his Peacemaker. There was a look on his face which sent a momentary chill through the two men facing him.

"Who the blazes are you?" asked Boyle.

"Name's Kilcane," said Dan. "I'm a friend of the Rennies. A friend who don't take kindly to seeing them bothered by the likes of you two. You'd better ride off now — and don't come back."

Boyle looked uncertainly at Dan. He felt uneasy about the stranger. Something told him that Dan would be a dangerous man to tangle with. He resisted the temptation to pull his gun.

"Ballard ain't going to like this!" he said.

"That's too bad," said Dan. "Just tell him he'll have to be satisfied with the range that he's got. He ain't got no right to turn homesteaders off their own land."

Boyle turned his horse, and rode off. Frazer followed suit.

Martha Rennie looked troubled, as she watched the two men leave.

"I'm wondering what's going to happen next," she said.

"It's hard to say," said Dan. "D'you know if Ballard's offered to buy anybody else out?"

"Not that I've heard of," she replied.

"I think I'll ride into town, and see the sheriff," said Dan. "I'd like to know where he stands in all this."

"Why are you doing this for us?" she asked. "It'd be a sight easier for you just to ride on, out of this valley, and forget all about what's happening here."

"Like I told you before," replied Dan, "I've got this interfering streak in me. It's caused me a lot of trouble in the past, but I can't seem to get rid of it. If I see something I don't like, I just can't help taking a hand to try to put things right.

"I'll ride into town now," he went on. "You got a rifle or shotgun in the house?"

She nodded, went inside, and returned with a Remington double-barrelled shotgun, and a box of cartridges. Dan inspected the shotgun, and loaded it with two cartridges.

"You know how to use this?" he asked.

"Yes," she replied. "John showed me a while ago."

"While I'm away," said Dan, "keep an eye out for visitors. I don't think Ballard's men will be bothering you again so soon, but if you see anybody you're not sure about, stay inside, near that window next to the door, and let them know you're holding a shotgun on them. And if they look like they're thinking of busting in, fire off a barrel. That should scare them off. I'll be back as soon as I can."

"I'll be all right," she said, and watched him for a while, as he rode down the valley. Then she went in to tell her husband what had happened.

When Dan reached Lorimer, his first call was at the livery stable. He went inside, and spoke to Dave Arnold.

"Did everything go all right this morning?" he asked. "The doctor ain't in any trouble?"

"No, he's all right," said Arnold. "Tracy knows that the doc was inside the house, when *he* was pistol-whipped on the stairs. When I pretended to find him early this morning, and cut him loose, he was sore as hell, what with that big bump on the back of his head, and being tied up all night, and lying in the dirt."

"Where is he now?" asked Dan.

"Still keeping an eye on the doc," replied Arnold.

Dan told Arnold what had happened back at the homestead, and said he was going to see the sheriff.

"Sheriff Brand is a bully," said Arnold. "And I'm pretty sure he's on Ballard's payroll. He won't do a thing without Ballard's say-so. He should never have been made county sheriff. Ballard got him the job somehow."

"All the same," said Dan. "I'll go along to see him. I'd be obliged," he went on, "if you'd let Doc Harper know that Rennie seems to be on the mend."

The Sheriff's Office was opposite to the bank. Dan walked his horse along to it, tied it to the hitching-rail, and went inside. Sheriff Brand was sitting back in his chair, his feet resting on the top of his desk. He was a man of average height, pot-bellied, with sparse, greying hair, and a florid complexion. He looked up at Dan. His expression was one of bored indifference.

"Yeah?" he said.

"I'm here," said Dan, "to report a breach of the law. There's a rancher called Ballard in this valley — I expect you know him — who's stopping the doctor from going out to a sick homesteader called Rennie, because he wants Rennie's land. Ballard says he won't let the doctor see Rennie till the land has been signed over to him. Seems to me you should bring this Ballard in, and explain the law to him."

Brand's feet crashed to the floor, and he sat bolt upright, then rose to his feet. His eyes were goggling.

"And who might you be?" he shouted.

"The name's Kilcane," said Dan.

"I'm a friend of the Rennies. First thing you'd better do, Sheriff, is to call off one of Ballard's men, name of Tracy, who's watching the doctor. Then you can take the doctor to see Rennie."

"Don't tell me what to do," shouted Brand, his face taking on an even more reddish hue. "I've a mind to put you in one of those cells."

"I'd think twice about that," said Dan, and there was something in his voice that rang a warning bell in Brand's mind. The sheriff backed down, but only slightly.

"What you're saying is a pack of lies," he said. "You got any witnesses?"

"Mrs Rennie for one," replied Dan. "And if you ask Doc Harper, he'll tell you that he ain't been able to get out to see Rennie. Ballard's men have seen to that."

"I'll look into it," said Brand, "but I'm sure that Mr Ballard either has a good reason for what his men are doing, or he doesn't know they're doing it."

"I guess what you're really saying, Sheriff," said Dan, "is that you ain't going to do a thing about it. I'm pretty sure now, that I know where you stand. You're with Ballard. And I'm warning you both, that if Ballard starts hassling any more homesteaders, he'll have a fight on his hands."

Brand, his face suffused with anger, went for his gun. He had barely lifted it from its holster, when Dan leaned over the desk, and jammed the long barrel of his Peacemaker hard into Brand's belly. The sheriff gasped, and dropped his six-gun back into its holster. Dan walked round the desk, took Brand's gun away from him, and threw it into the far corner of the room. Then he walked out to his horse.

He headed straight for the Rennie homestead. Martha Rennie came out of the house as he rode up. She seemed relieved to see him. She told him she had seen no riders since he left for Lorimer.

Over the next two weeks, Rennie's

condition steadily improved, and the time came when he was fit to start work around the homestead again. There had been no further sign of Ballard's men near any of the homesteads.

"I know everything's quiet," said Dan to the Rennies, "but I can't help thinking that what we're seeing is the lull before the storm. Ballard ain't going to give up that easy."

The day after Dan made this prediction, he was standing outside the house with Rennie, when a homesteader called Hank Horton, riding fast, came up to the house. He was a married man, without children, with a homestead located halfway into town from the Rennie place.

Dan had already gathered from Rennie that among the homesteaders, there was a tacit recognition of Horton as their leader. All three men went into the house.

"It's bad news," said Horton. "You know that Chuck Newton has the place next to mine, and he just finished that new timber house a week ago, and moved in. Well, he woke up in the middle of the night, to find that the house was on fire. He and his wife got out just in time. The house was burnt right down. There were clear signs outside that somebody had started the fire on purpose."

"Did Newton tell the sheriff?" asked Rennie.

"He did," replied Horton, "and Brand rode out to the homestead, and had a look round. Then he said he'd look around for tracks. I asked him if he wanted any help, but he said he didn't. So I left him. My guess is, that if it's left to Brand to find out who did it, he'll come up with nothing. Just now, I'm riding round all the homesteaders, to tell them to be on their guard. After all those threats Ballard's men have been shouting at us, I figure he's responsible."

"I think you're right," said Rennie, and he told Horton how Ballard's men had tried to stop the doctor from coming to see him.

"If you don't mind a stranger butting in," said Dan, "you homesteaders really should get yourselves organized against Ballard. If you don't, he'll just pick you off, one by one, until the ones who're left are so scared, they'll all move out together. I've seen it happen in other places. And it'll keep on happening till the law spreads a lot wider than it is now, and till we get more law officers who do their job like it ought to be done, and don't take money to turn a blind eye when the law's being broken."

"You sound as if you've come up against this sort of thing before," said Horton.

"My father had a homestead near Ogallala, in Nebraska," said Dan. "I joined the Union Army, and stayed on as a lieutenant when the war ended. Then I got news that my father had been lynched by vigilantes, who claimed he'd rustled some cattle. The branded cattle had been planted in his pasture

32

during the night, and the vigilantes had been organized by a cattleman called Stewart.

"I got my discharge as soon as I could," Dan went on, "and went back to Ogallala. I found my mother was half-crazed, on account of she saw my father hanged. She died soon after I got back. It took a long time, but with the help of a U.S. Marshal I knew, I got the proof that my father was innocent, and that Stewart was responsible for his death. Stewart and the vigilantes were hanged soon after."

"I'm sorry about your parents," said Horton, "and I can see why you're worried about the situation here. What I'd better do, is call all the homesteaders together, so we can talk about this, and decide what to do. Looks like we can't expect any help from the sheriff."

He looked at Dan. "You'd be welcome to sit in," he said. "Maybe you can give us some good advice."

"I'd be glad to," said Dan. "How

many homesteads are there altogether?"

"Nineteen," replied Horton. "Nine this side of town, ten on the other side. We all came out in the same wagon train. None of us did any fighting in the war.

"I'd best be leaving now," he went on. "I'm going to get as many men from the homesteads together as I can. We'll all meet at my place at seven o'clock this evening."

When Dan and Rennie arrived at the Horton homestead just before seven that evening, there was already a sizeable crowd of men in Horton's living-room. A few more settlers came in while Rennie was introducing Dan to those present.

Dan glanced around the assembly, as Horton was getting ready to address them. He could see that the majority of the men looked to be in their forties, only three of them appearing to be appreciably older than the rest. As Horton started speaking, the conversation died down.

"You all know why we're here," he said. "Ballard's starting to move in on us. He stopped the doctor from going out to see John here, when he took sick, and there ain't much doubt it was him had Chuck's house burnt down. And Chuck and his wife might have died in that fire. Question is, what are we going to do about it, seeing as we ain't got no law to turn to? We all know, it ain't no use going to the sheriff.

"It seems to me," he continued, "that we either quit everything we've built up here, and look for a quarter section somewhere else, where exactly the same sort of thing might happen again, or, we get ourselves organized, and start standing up to Ballard and his men. I'd like to know how everybody feels about this."

He paused, and looked around the gathering, then waited, as a buzz of conversation arose. After a while, one of the men, a homesteader called Chris Catlin, spoke out. He was one of the three older men present. "Standing up to Ballard ain't going to be that easy," he said. "His hands are all a bit more than cowboys. They all wear guns, and look like they know how to use them. And from what I hear, he has at least twenty hands just now. I reckon some of them are hand-picked for the job of clearing us out of the valley. But this is fine farming land we've got here, with water close by, and I sure don't aim to lose it without a fight."

There was a murmur of assent from the other homesteaders. Then another settler spoke up.

"I agree with Chris," he said, "but if we ain't careful, some of us are going to get killed. How do we take Ballard on, and still make sure nobody on our side is going to get hurt? Everybody knows we ain't fighting men. We're farmers."

Horton spoke again.

"I've told you all about Mr Kilcane's father and mother," he said, "and about the rancher who ordered the lynching, and what happened to him.

I asked Mr Kilcane to come along here, because I thought maybe he'd be able to tell us the best way of dealing with Ballard. We'd be obliged for any advice you can give us, Mr Kilcane."

"What's starting to happen here," said Dan, "has already happened in other places. The first thing to do, is to get yourselves organized, and pick a leader. It's not going to be easy, but you've got to try and be ready for any move that Ballard makes. He's got the advantage that most of his men are probably used to gunplay and violence, while you homesteaders ain't in the habit of even wearing a sidearm. I guess you've all got rifles that you've used now and again for shooting rabbits and prairie dogs and suchlike, but shooting men and game are two different things. You've got to get in some shooting practice as quick as you can, and you've got to get used to the idea that you might have to use those rifles against Ballard's men.

"And if the time comes when you

have to do that," Dan continued, "those rifles have got to be in good condition, with plenty of ammunition around for when it's needed. And the same goes for any pistols and shotguns you might have. As for casualties, nobody can guarantee that none of you will get hurt. Maybe it'll be the price you have to pay for staying in the valley. You're all strong and determined men, or you'd never have made it out here in the first place. But I guess that some of you will start worrying about your wives and children, and will feel that maybe it would be best to move on.

"Each one of you will have to make up his own mind about that," Dan continued, "but it's clear that the more of you there are here, the less chance Ballard has of driving you out."

When Dan had finished speaking, Horton left his side, and went over to talk to the settlers, who grouped around him, out of earshot of Dan. After a fairly lengthy discussion, Horton came back to Dan.

"Everybody feels the same," he said. "They want to stay. But they figure they'd stand a lot better chance of getting the better of Ballard, if you'd agree to take charge of the operation. They know about your service in the Cavalry. They're all willing to chip in, and give you a reasonable wage. And Rennie would like you to stay on at his place for the time being, if that's what you want. What d'you say?"

"I'll do what you want," replied Dan, "because Ballard shouldn't be allowed to get his own way over this. But I don't want no pay. All I want is that you settlers do just what I tell you to do. Otherwise, we'll get nowhere. We've got to have discipline if we're going to beat Ballard.

"And one other thing," he went on, "I'm going to send for a friend, to give me a hand. He was my sergeant in the Cavalry. Name of Jack McLaren.

He left the Army same time as I did. I know he's at a loose end just now, staying at his father's ranch in Colorado. This job's going to be a lot easier if he and I can work on it together."

Horton went over to talk for a while with the other settlers. Then he came back to Dan.

"We'll all do what you say," he said. "Will you talk to us now, and give us some idea of what you're planning to do?"

"Sure," said Dan.

Speaking to the homesteaders, he told them they should avoid going into town alone. It would be better if two or three families went in together. Everybody should keep a sharp lookout all the time, getting the children to help out in the daytime, if they were old enough. If any homesteader saw a group of riders approaching his house, he should fire off three rifle shots, to alert his neighbours.

At night-time, Dan told them, until

they could set up an alarm system, they should keep a watch all night, members of a family taking it in turns, in case there was an attempt at arson, or break-in. But they should keep watch from inside the house, with doors and windows securely fastened, and should fire at any intruders.

"Those are the basic things to do," said Dan. "I'll ride round to all your places soon, to have a look at your firearms, and your door and window fastenings and to talk about that alarm system. But tomorrow, first thing, I'm going to ride out on the range, to look it over. I've got to think of some way to carry the fight to Ballard when it really starts up.

"I expect we'll have a day or two without trouble," he went on, "while Ballard waits to see what your reaction is to the fire. He'll be waiting to see if the Newtons show any signs of leaving."

After some of the settlers had arranged to get together the following day, to make a start on rebuilding Chuck Newton's house, they left for their homesteads. Dan returned with Rennie, and went into the barn, to get some sleep.

3

DAN woke early the following morning, and after breakfast he rode to the Telegraph Office in town, and sent a message to Jack McLaren, on his father's ranch. Then he left town, and rode south, past the homesteads, and along the eastern boundary of Ballard's range, keeping a close watch for Circle B riders. Eventually, he crossed the boundary, and climbed out of the valley to the high ground which bordered it. He found himself on rough terrain, with little vegetation. It was mostly flat, but was studded with several large rock outcrops ahead. He rode towards these, and just after passing between two of them, he suddenly came upon a large, deep hollow, not visible from a distance. He rode down into it, and almost at its centre, close to a large boulder, he reined in his mount, as he saw in front of him a hole in the ground, about five feet in diameter.

He dismounted, walked up to the edge of the hole, and peered down into it. His eyes, accustomed to the bright light outside, could distinguish nothing down inside the pit, but he could see that the hole widened below the surface of the ground.

He picked up a large stone, dropped it through the side of the hole nearest to him, and heard it strike something below. From the time interval before the stone hit, he made a rough guess that it had dropped about fifteen feet. He dropped another rock through the opposite side of the hole, and got a similar result.

He took his lariat from his horse, tied knots along its length, then fastened one end off around the boulder close to the hole, and dropped the other end into the pit. He started to climb down the rope, and paused when he had descended about ten feet. Listening, he could hear the sound of running water. He descended a few more feet, until the soles of his boots touched a level surface. Still holding the rope, he stood motionless, letting his eyes grow accustomed to the darkness.

Outside the sun was high in the sky. A shaft of sunlight passing through the entrance to the pit illuminated part of the inside, providing sufficient light to show Dan that the floor was roughly circular, with a diameter of about nine yards, and that the roof of the pit was high enough to allow him to walk around the floor, erect. He could see a stream of water running across the floor.

Wishing to examine the pit more closely, he started to walk around, striking matches where necessary. He saw no signs of live animals, but he saw the skeletons of several small ones, which must have fallen into the pit in the past. He also found the two narrow tunnels, where the running water entered and left the pit.

He climbed up the rope, retrieved it, then rode up to an area covered with tall brush, close to the steep side of the hollow. Closely skirting the brush, he glanced into it, and stopped. He thought he could see a partly-hidden structure of some sort. He dismounted, and walked into the brush, towards the object which had caught his eye. It was a small log cabin, almost completely overgrown. Close by, was a small freshwater spring.

Forcing a way through to the door, Dan pushed it open and went inside. It was obvious that the cabin had not been occupied for a long time. There was a stove, and basic furniture, in reasonable condition, and the structure looked to be quite sound, despite its neglected appearance.

Dan went back to his horse, and rode out of the hollow. Looking back, he could see that to a rider on the rim of the hollow, neither the pit nor the shack would be discernible. He rode back to the Rennie homestead, seeing nobody on the way.

Early the following morning, Dan went to the store in town, and bought several large bundles of strong twine, and a quantity of U-shaped wire staples, of the type suitable for fixing wire to fence posts. Then he rode to the first homestead north of town, and checked the weapons, then the door and window fastenings.

Then, with the homesteader, a man called Watkins, Dan constructed a simple alarm system, which would give warning of anyone approaching the house during the hours of darkness. They cut a number of short, thin wooden stakes, and hammered these firmly into the ground, to form a circle around the house. Then, into the top of each stake, they hammered a U-shaped staple, and threaded a length of twine through the staples.

They took the two ends of twine into the house, through a hole made in the wall, up to, and through, a staple in the ceiling, and halfway down to the floor, where they were tied to a piece of wood, just sufficiently heavy to keep the twine taut. Several empty tin cans were tied, close together, to the lengths of twine dropping vertically from the ceiling. Outside, the twine was about four inches above ground level. When tested, the device worked perfectly. Any foot contact with the twine outside produced a jangle from the cans inside the house.

"If anybody does come in the night, with the idea of setting fire to the house, or breaking in," said Dan, "you should be able to stop them before they do any damage. If that alarm sounds, fire a few shots from the windows, even if you can't see anybody, and I figure that'll scare them away. But keep the inside of the house dark, and don't go outside.

"At daybreak," he went on, "dismantle the alarm, and put it back on again at nightfall."

Dan briefly visited the remaining homesteads, checked their weapons and security, handed over some twine and staples, and explained how to set up the alarm system. By the time he got back to the Rennie homestead, it was late in the evening.

The following morning, the homesteader Horton rode up while Dan and the Rennies were having breakfast. He told them that there had been two incidents during the night. At his own place, around one in the morning, the alarm had been triggered, and he had fired towards two shadowy figures, barely distinguishable in the dark. Both figures had quickly retreated, and there was no further attempt to approach the house.

The second incident, similar in nature, had occurred an hour later, at the Catlin homestead, north of town. Here, the intruders had come under fire from both Catlin and his wife, and had been forced to beat a hasty retreat. But on this occasion, they had left behind a full can of coal oil, giving evidence of their intention.

There was no evidence that any of the intruders had been hit.

Later in the day, Dan decided to ride into Lorimer, but on this occasion he crossed the river, at a shallow point close to the Rennie homestead, and headed north for Lorimer, across Circle B range. He had ridden a couple of miles, when he saw a rider ahead, and to his left, on a converging path. The rider was moving fast, and was apparently, like himself, heading for town. Keeping his eyes on the rider, Dan saw the horse suddenly lurch sideways, stagger forward a few paces, and roll over on to its side. The rider was thrown off, and lay motionless, close to the horse.

Dan urged his horse into a gallop, and headed for the fallen mount. Reaching it, he dismounted, and ran to the rider. She was a woman in her twenties, lying on her side, her eyes closed, wearing a black riding skirt, and coloured shirt. A black, broad-brimmed hat lay on the ground beside her. She was of medium height, slim, with shoulder-length dark hair, and, even in her distress, so good-looking, that, for a moment, Dan's breath was taken away.

She appeared to be unconscious, and Dan could see that her left foot and part of her left leg below the knee, were trapped under the horse's left shoulder. The animal was making tentative efforts to get up. Quickly, Dan took off his vest, and put it over the horse's eyes, to quieten the animal. Then he examined it closely. It was clear that there was a fracture, high up on the left foreleg. He drew his Peacemaker, and shot the mare through the head.

Tying his lariat around the dead horse's neck, he fastened the other end to his own saddle horn. He urged his horse forward, and as it started to pull, the weight was lifted from the woman's leg, then the dead horse was dragged clear of her.

Dan ran back to the woman, and saw

that she was coming round. As her dark eyes opened, she shook her head, then looked at the dead mare, and up at Dan, who was standing over her.

"What happened?" she asked.

"You took a bad fall when your mare went down," replied Dan, "and your horse broke a foreleg. I had to shoot it."

"Yes, I remember falling, now," she said. "I think she stepped in a hole."

"As well as falling off your horse, the horse fell on your foot and leg," said Dan. "I pulled it off you as quick as I could. D'you feel as if you've got any broken bones?"

She moved her arms, then her right and left legs. As she moved her left leg, she gave a cry of pain.

"My left leg," she said. "Feels like it's been damaged low down. But I don't think anything's broken. Feels more like it's been crushed. Otherwise, apart from a few bruises, I reckon I'm all right."

Dan looked at the sturdy, almost

knee-length boots she was wearing.

"I figure it'll be safer to leave your boot on till I get you to the doctor," he said. "It ain't far into town."

He lifted her on to his horse, climbed up in front of her, and headed for Lorimer.

"You all right?" he asked over his shoulder, after they had covered a quarter of a mile.

"I'm all right," she replied. "Better introduce myself. I'm Mary Ballard. My father owns the Circle B. I'm sure grateful you were riding this way today."

"I'm Dan Kilcane," said Dan. "Glad I happened by."

He had seen the brand on the girl's horse, and had already guessed that she was Ballard's daughter. He wondered if she knew of, and approved, her father's treatment of the homesteaders.

When they reached town, Dan rode up to the building where the doctor lived, dismounted, climbed the stairs, and knocked on the door. When Harper opened it, Dan went down for the woman, and carried her up the steps, and into a small room at the back, where he laid her on a bed.

"What happened, Mary?" asked Harper.

She told him about the fall, and pointed to her left leg.

"I think this has been damaged," she said. "It's hurting some."

Harper looked at the boot on her left foot.

"I'll have to cut that boot off," he said.

Taking a sharp knife from a drawer, he carefully slit the boot leather from top to bottom, eased the boot off, and closely examined the woman's lower leg and foot.

"I'm pretty sure," he said, when he had finished, "that there's no fracture. But I think there's a ligament injury of the ankle. It's got to be rested for two or three weeks. I'll put a bandage on it now.

"Remember," he said, when he had

done this, "it's *got* to be rested, or it just won't get better. I'll run you home now in my buggy. I'll go . . . " He stopped short, then continued: "Darn it! I've just remembered. I've got one of the homesteaders coming here in about half an hour from now, for some treatment that can't wait."

"I'd be glad to take Miss Ballard out to the ranch, if the buggy's free," offered Dan.

"It's free," said Harper, and looked at Mary.

"I'd be grateful, Mr Kilcane," she said, "if it's not going to interfere with anything else you were going to do."

"Nothing that can't wait," said Dan.

The doctor went to the livery stable for his horse and buggy, and when he returned, Dan carried the woman out to it, and sat her inside. Then he climbed on to the seat of the buggy, beside her.

"Don't forget what I said, Mary, about resting that ankle," the doctor called out as they were leaving. "Send for me if it don't seem to be getting any better."

They sat in silence for a while, as Dan drove the buggy out of town, at a moderate pace. He asked her if the ankle was very painful.

"Not so bad, with this bandage on," she replied. "So long as I keep it still. Lucky this buggy's well-sprung.

"You living in this valley, Mr Kilcane?" she asked. "I don't remember seeing you around before."

"No, I don't live here permanent," he replied. "I was just planning to ride through, then I changed my mind, and thought I'd like to hang around for a spell."

"I can understand that," she said. "I love Wyoming. It's a beautiful Territory. I've just spent some time with relatives in Iowa. I went there when my mother died. It's what they call more civilized back there, but I couldn't wait to get back to Wyoming."

Dan didn't tell her that it wasn't the scenery that was holding him in the valley. He wondered if she knew anything of her father's plans to move the homesteaders out.

"This valley sure is a fine place to settle in," said Dan. "If I wanted a homestead, this is where I'd like to be. I've had a look at some of the crops on those homesteads on the other side of the river, and it's clear that it's good land for farming."

"Yes," she said. "I'd like to get to know some of the women on the homesteads. I miss female company. But for some reason, my father doesn't like the idea.

"He reckons it's fine cattle-raising country, too," she went on. "He's talking of bringing more cattle in before long."

"He's got enough range here to expand his herd, then?" asked Dan.

"He must have," she replied. "There ain't many who know more about cattle-raising than father."

Dan was sure now that the woman knew nothing of her father's activities against the homesteaders.

They continued in silence, until they were approaching the ranch buildings. A tall windmill stood not far from the ranch-house, outside which two men were standing, watching the approaching buggy. One of the men Dan recognized as Ballard's foreman, Boyle, one of the two men who had been at the Rennie homestead when Dan first arrived there. The other man was stocky, of medium height, and bearded.

"That's father," said the woman. "He's the one with the beard."

As the buggy drew closer to the house Boyle said something to Ballard, then both men walked to meet it. Dan pulled up as they reached him.

"Mary!" said Ballard. "What's happened?"

She told him about the fall, her visit to the doctor, and Dan's part in the proceedings. Ballard looked at Dan.

"I'll carry my daughter in," he said.

"Then I'd like a few words with you."

"I'll wait," said Dan, getting down from the buggy and watching as the rancher lifted his daughter out and carried her into the house. Boyle went with him.

Fifteen minutes later, the two men came out of the house. Boyle walked over to the bunkhouse, and Ballard approached Dan. The rancher had a hard, cruel face, with black, beetling eyebrows. He was scowling as he came to a stop in front of Dan.

"Keep away from my daughter, Kilcane," he said. "I've heard about you. You're a troublemaker. There ain't no place for you in this valley. If you're wise, you'll ride out before you gets hurt."

"About your daughter," said Dan, "If she tells me herself to keep away from her, that's what I'll do. As for troublemaking, seems to me you've being doing a lot of that yourself lately. Before you came into this valley, the homesteaders got on fine with the man who was running this ranch before you. Seems it was a bad day for them when you took over."

Ballard's scowl deepened. His face flushed.

"Barrett was a weak fool," he said. "The range in this valley is just right for cattle-raising. It's wasted on farmers. Those settlers are just going to have to get out."

"You've no right to force them out," said Dan, "and you know it. The land they're on is theirs by right of settlement."

Ballard glared at Dan.

"They'll have to leave in the end," he said, harshly. "It's up to them whether they accept a reasonable price for their holdings, and leave peaceable-like, or whether they act awkward, and run into a whole heap of trouble, and still have to leave in the end.

"And as for you," he went on, "I'm warning you again. Stop interfering in my affairs. Keep away from my daughter. And get out of this valley."

60

Ballard turned, and stomped angrily back into the house. Dan stood looking after him for a moment, then climbed into the buggy, and set off towards town.

4

THE following day Dan paid another visit to the sheriff. Brand, seated at his desk, stiffened as Dan walked in.

"I've spoken to Ballard," he said, quickly, before Dan could speak. "He reckoned that his men were acting on their own when they stopped the doctor going to see Rennie. He's told them if they step out of line again, they'll be sacked."

"That's hard to believe," said Dan, "but let's pass on to the fire at the Newton homestead that you're looking into. You managed to solve that one yet?"

"I'm working on it," said Brand. "Can't find any proof that some outsider was responsible. Looks like maybe Newton or his wife was careless with a lamp, or the stove."

"But how about the other two homesteads that were visited in the night?" asked Dan. "It was clear that if those intruders hadn't been chased off, they'd have fired one of the houses at least. They left a can of coal oil behind, when they left."

Brand looked startled.

"I can see that Ballard ain't bothered to tell you how his men got chased off," said Dan.

Brand ignored Dan's remark.

"If there's been more trouble out there, I should've been told, when it happened," he said.

"I didn't tell you, because I figured it wouldn't do any good," said Dan.

"You figured," said Brand. "How come a stranger like you's taking a hand in this?"

"Because the homesteaders asked me to help them to stand up to Ballard," replied Dan. "That's why. And that's what I've agreed to do.

"I've got some advice for you, Brand," he went on. "You can take it from me, the homesteaders are going to win this battle against Ballard. It's something I'm going to see to personally. And if it comes out that you've sided with Ballard in breaking the law, I'm going to see to it that you're in real trouble. So you'd better think good about where you're going to stand in this business."

Dan left the Sheriff's Office, leaving behind him a man a little worried at first, but soon reassuring himself that Ballard would quickly deal with this troublesome stranger.

The next three days passed without any unusual incidents. Dan spent his time working around the homestead. Rennie, now much improved, was performing a few light tasks. In the late afternoon of the third day, they were together in the cornfield, when they saw a horse and rider coming from the direction of town. Even at that distance, they could see that the rider was a big man. Dan watched him for a while, then turned to Rennie.

"We're in luck," he said. "That rider coming this way is my old friend, ex-Sergeant Jack McLaren. I told you I was sending for him. We served together during the war, and for a while after. Jack McLaren was a fine soldier, and he's a fine man, and just like a brother to me. He's absolutely reliable, strong as an ox, and a great man in a fight. He's a good tracker, too, and one of the best Indian fighters I've ever met. He can move like a shadow in the dark. He saved my life when we were fighting the Sioux warrior Crazy Horse near Fort Phil Kearny. I was wounded bad, and our horses had run off. He carried me five miles, back to the fort."

The oncoming rider raised a large hand in greeting, as he recognized Dan, who had walked with Rennie to the edge of the field. He came to a stop as he reached them, and dismounted. He wore a Colt .45 in a right-hand holster, and a knife in his belt. He was a shade over six feet in height, strongly built, with massive shoulders, and in his early thirties. He wore a neat black moustache There was a broad grin on his deeply-tanned face as he walked up to Dan.

"Reporting for duty, Dan," he said, then shook hands, first with Dan, then with Rennie, as the latter was introduced to him.

"What sort of a hole have you got yourself into this time, Dan?" asked Jack. "Must be pretty bad for you to have to send for your old sergeant to give you a helping hand."

He turned to Rennie.

"This is nothing new, Mr Rennie," he said. "When we were fighting the Sioux together, Dan was always thinking up new ways of getting himself into trouble, and who was it who had to sort out the mess? Why, dependable young Sergeant McLaren, of course."

"Shut up, Jack," grinned Dan. "Let me tell you exactly what the situation is here."

He told Jack of all that had transpired

since his own arrival at the Rennie homestead.

"And now," he went on, "we're all keeping watch, and waiting to see what Ballard's next move will be."

"Good," said Jack. "Glad I got here before the real action started."

Dan turned to Rennie.

"Can we both stay in the barn here for the time being?" he asked.

"Sure," replied Rennie. "Glad to have you. And any meals you want here, Martha says you're very welcome."

After supper, Dan and Jack sat in the barn for a while, chatting about old comrades, and their life in the Cavalry. It was almost midnight before they finally turned in.

The following morning they had just finished breakfast and were leaving the house when they saw a rider approaching fast, from the direction of town. He turned on to the homestead, and dismounted as he reached them. It was Horton. He looked curiously at Jack, and Dan introduced the two men.

Then Horton spoke to Dan.

"Looks like Ballard is on the move again," he said. "Henry Frost and his wife and their seven-year old daughter went missing during the night, and his two horses are missing from the pasture. Maybe you remember that Henry's homestead lies between mine and town. He was seen by a neighbour yesterday evening, but he and his wife and daughter were all missing when the same man called by arrangement, at dawn. And the door had been broken down.

"For some reason," Horton went on, "Henry hadn't connected up his alarm, and it looked like somebody had sneaked up to the house and knocked the door down before Henry could fire on them."

"Ballard must be behind this," said Dan. "Did anybody hear any shots?"

"No," replied Horton.

"There was no message in the house?" asked Dan.

Horton shook his head.

"We'll go back with you to Frost's homestead," said Dan, "and we'll see if we can follow the tracks made when Ballard's men were taking the Frosts away. We're lucky Jack's here to give us a hand. There ain't many better, when it comes to tracking."

When they reached Frost's homestead, Dan and Horton held back while Jack dismounted, then closely examined the ground in the vicinity of the house and the narrow track leading from the house to the main track running outside the homestead boundary. Then he went inside the house. When he emerged, a short while later, he walked over to Dan and Horton.

"As far as I can tell," he said, "three men rode in during the night, and left their horses near the barn there. Then they went over to the house on foot, and broke in. They must have knocked down the door so quickly that Frost didn't have a chance to fire his rifle. It's lying on the table, fully loaded.

"They came out of the house," Jack

went on, "with the Frosts and their daughter. They walked over to the three horses, then one of them brought two horses from the pasture, and the five horses headed off the homestead. I figure that Frost and his daughter were probably on the same horse. My guess is, they left here in the middle of the night. It weren't all that dark last night. There was plenty of light for them to ride by."

"Jack and I are going to follow those tracks," said Dan to Horton. "You'd better tell the other homesteaders what's happened here. Tell them to make sure they set their alarm systems at night, and tell them I think it would be a good idea now for them to set up a night watch from inside the house."

"I'll do that," said Horton. "Where d'you think Ballard's men are taking the Frosts?"

"That's hard to say," replied Dan. "But we've got one thing to be thankful for. Ballard hasn't quite reached the killing stage yet. Otherwise, Frost would have been murdered on his homestead. Ballard is still trying to intimidate you and the others, hoping you'll decide to move out. You and the others had better keep an eye on Frost's place. Maybe Ballard'll get the idea that while there's nobody there, this is a good time to burn the buildings down."

"We'll do the best we can," said Horton.

Dan and Jack followed the tracks of the five horses off the homestead, and continued to follow them as they crossed the river, swung south, and headed up the valley. The tracks did not run in a straight line, and Jack and Dan had the feeling that the horses had been taken on a course which would make it difficult to follow them.

Progress was slow, but Jack's tracking skills brought them eventually to a point about five miles from the homestead, where the five horses had stopped for a while. Jack dismounted, and closely studied the jumble of tracks.

"One of the riders left the others,

and headed northwest," he said.

"Probably going to the ranch-house," said Dan.

"The other four horses kept on heading south," said Jack.

"Looks like Ballard's decided to start moving the settlers out of the valley by force," said Dan. "Let's hope he hasn't harmed the Frosts."

They followed the tracks left by the four horses, and eventually they found themselves leaving the Circle B range, and climbing up the head of the valley, towards a gap in the range of hills cutting across their path. They had just reached the highest point in the pass, when Jack shouted to Dan to follow him into the shelter of a large boulder standing at one side of the pass.

"Two riders, about a mile ahead," he said, "coming this way."

They led their horses up the side of the pass, into a crevice from which they could, unobserved, watch the track below.

When the riders came into view,

they were close enough for Dan to recognize the nearest one instantly. It was Tracy, the Circle B hand who had been ordered by Ballard to prevent the doctor from visiting Rennie. The other rider was a stranger to Dan. They waited until the two riders had passed out of sight. Then they continued to follow the tracks of the four horses.

They caught up with Henry and Rebecca Frost and their daughter Jane in mid-afternoon. They were sitting, rather forlornly, in a small grassy hollow, with a pool of water at its centre. The two horses were grazing nearby. The Frosts stood up as they saw the two approaching riders. They recognized Dan as he drew closer.

"You all right?" asked Dan, as he dismounted, and saw the ugly bruise and swelling on the side of Frost's head.

"They pistol-whipped me back at the homestead," said Frost, "but they haven't harmed Rebecca and Jane. They brought us well out of the valley, and told us if we turned round, and tried to get back on to Circle B range, there were men waiting at the pass who'd shoot us down on sight, and bury us where we fell. They've given us just enough provisions to get us to the next town south of here. Didn't you meet up with them on the way out here?"

"We saw them," said Dan, "but they didn't see us. And they headed right through the pass, and into the valley. And we didn't see any more men around there. I guess they were just bluffing when they said that Circle B hands would be watching out for you at the pass."

"Maybe so," said Frost. "We stopped here," he explained, "to rest for a spell. We've been riding a long time."

Dan introduced Jack, thought for a moment, then spoke to the Frosts.

"What we'd like to do," he said, "is take you back to your homestead. If we travel through the night, I reckon there's a good chance of us getting there without Circle B men seeing us. The other homesteaders are keeping an eye on your place while you're away. When we get back, we've got to get organized, to try and make sure Ballard doesn't do this sort of thing again.

"We can't guarantee," Dan went on, "that nobody'll get hurt, but Jack and me'll do our best to stop that happening."

As Frost turned to his wife, he saw the look of grim determination on her face.

"What d'you think, Rebecca?" he asked her.

"All the things we've worked and slaved for for years, are back at that homestead," she said, "and a lot of them travelled with us in a covered wagon for nigh on a thousand miles. You can't expect me to leave them all behind without a fight. I'm surprised you thought you had to ask me, Henry Frost. Let's be on our way back, just as soon as we can. When we get home, I've a good mind to get me a shotgun, and go after Ballard myself."

Frost smiled. He looked at his wife, fondly.

"You can see what a hell-cat I married," he said to Dan and Jack. "But she's dead right. We're going back, and we're mighty obliged to you for coming after us."

"Right," said Dan. "We'll rest here for a while, and let the horses graze. We'll have a good meal, and set off for the valley just before dark. The three men'll take turns carrying Jane."

5

THEY reached the Frost homestead, without incident, just as
dawn was breaking. It appeared,
from the outside, to be just as it was
when the Frosts had left it the previous
day. As Frost approached the door of
the house, a voice came from inside.

"This is Horton," it shouted. "I'm
coming out."

A moment later, Horton appeared in
the doorway.

"Saw it was you, through the
window," he said. "I sure am glad
to see you back. We've been keeping
an eye on your place. We haven't had
somebody here all the time, but we've
done the best we could."

Frost thanked Horton, and told him
what had happened since Ballard's men
had taken him away. Then he went into
the house with his wife and daughter.

"Has there been any more trouble since Jack and I left?" Dan asked Horton.

"Nope," replied Horton.

"It's not going to be long," said Dan, "before Ballard finds out that the Frosts are back, and that's probably when he'll make his next move. I guess he figured that when the Frosts disappeared like that, maybe some of the other homesteaders would get really scared, and move out themselves.

"Meanwhile," he went on, "you'd better all carry on keeping a close watch for Ballard's men."

"Right," said Horton, "and I'll let all the homesteaders know that the Frosts are safe, and back home."

The following day, Dan and Jack rode into town. Dan wanted a few things from the store. On the outskirts of town, they caught up with the Frost and Rennie families, on their buckboards, and accompanied them up to the store. Looking towards the saloon, Dan saw the Circle B foreman,

Boyle, come out through the swing doors, closely followed by Tracy.

Tracy stopped short as he saw the Frosts, and his jaw dropped. He stared at them, as though he could not believe his eyes. Then he spoke urgently to Boyle, who looked over at the homesteaders, and Dan and Jack. The two Circle B men turned, and went back into the saloon.

Dan and Jack went into the store, and looked round while the storekeeper Sam Blair, and his wife Ellen, were tending to the homesteaders. Blair was a small, pleasant man, middle-aged and sandy-haired. It was a spacious store, with plenty of room for moving round to examine the goods on the shelves.

When the homesteaders had made their purchases, they left the store, and Dan watched through a window as they climbed on their buckboards, turned them, and headed out of town. Dan glanced over at the saloon. As he did so, Boyle came through the doors, followed by four men. They were Tracy and Frazer, and two men called Whitman and Barstow, whom Dan hadn't seen before. Whitman was a big, swarthy-complexioned man, showing a fair amount of excess fat around his middle. There was a look on his face that indicated he was spoiling for a fight. Barstow was smaller, and looked equally ready for trouble.

All five men stepped off the boardwalk into the street, bunched up, and walked towards the store, in a purposeful sort of way. Dan called to Jack, who was at the counter.

"Company on the way," he said. "Circle B foreman and four men. Don't think it's a friendly visit."

Sam Blair looked startled, then stared at the door, as Boyle came in, followed by his companions. They stopped just inside the door, closing it behind them, and stood side by side, facing Dan and Jack, who were standing together, their backs to the counter.

Boyle spoke to Dan. His voice was harsh.

"You've been told to get out of this valley, Kilcane," he said, "but it seems like you're too bull-headed to take any notice. And you're still meddling in matters that ain't no concern of yours. So we figure to make it absolutely clear to you that you ain't wanted here. There ain't no need for gunplay. I reckon we can make you see reason without that."

He spoke to Jack.

"I don't know who *you* are, stranger," he said, "but maybe you'd better part company with Kilcane right now. You'll be a lot safer outside."

"What, and miss all the fun," said Jack. "I can't wait to get my hands on old pot-belly there," he gestured towards Whitman.

Whitman snarled, his face suffused with rage, and he restrained himself with difficulty from advancing on Jack. He waited impatiently for Boyle to give the word.

"Have it your way," said Boyle, to Jack.

"Mr Boyle," said the storekeeper, "can't you settle this out in the street? You could do a lot of damage in here."

"I figure we can handle this better inside," said Boyle. "These men have got to be taught a lesson. Mr Ballard will pay for any damage done."

The five men advanced slowly on Dan and Jack, who stepped apart, and a little forward from the counter. Then Tracy and Frazer moved in fast on Dan, and Whitman and Barstow rushed at Jack. Boyle stayed behind, to observe the proceedings.

Dan executed a quick sidestep, to evade the two men advancing on him, and punched Tracy on the side of the head with such force that the Circle B man cannoned into his partner Frazer, who was by his side. Frazer tripped, and fell on the floor, and Tracy, dazed, fell on top of him. Frazer squirmed from underneath Tracy, stepped over him, and advanced on Dan again, arms flailing. Dan easily avoided a flurry of wild punches, then slipped in an accurately-targeted punch, with all his strength behind it, which slammed on to the side of Frazer's jaw. Frazer's legs gave way, and he fell heavily on top of Tracy, who was making a feeble attempt to get up.

Meanwhile, Jack moved quickly up to Whitman and Barstow, and roughly pushed Barstow, a small man, to one side, so that, momentarily, he was face to face with Whitman alone. Whitman's fists were up, ready to smash into Jack's face, but Jack dropped his head before the blows could connect, and delivered two powerful, right-hand punches, with all his weight behind them, which sank deep into the pit of Whitman's unguarded stomach. Whitman's face twisted in agony, and he sank to the floor, clutching his middle, as Barstow came at Jack from the side.

Evading Barstow's fists, Jack struck him twice across the face, very hard, with his open hand, and before the dazed Circle B hand could recover,

Jack grasped him by the scruff of the neck and one leg, lifted him up in the air, and launched him at Boyle, who, having just decided it was time for him to enter into the fray, was moving towards Jack.

Boyle, falling awkwardly, crashed to the floor, with Barstow on top of him, and yelled out with pain, as his left shoulder dislocated. Barstow got shakily to his feet, but he would have done better to stay down. He squared up to Jack, but once again he was grasped, hoisted high in the air, and this time, was thrown forcibly on top of Whitman, who was still doubled up on the floor. The two men's heads collided, and Barstow lay still.

Jack glanced over at Dan, just in time to see Tracy, who had got up from the floor, go down to a second punch to the head. This time, he lay still.

Dan and Jack, breathing heavily, stood side by side for a while, looking at the five men on the floor. They were all conscious now, but none of them seemed anxious to get up. Boyle was holding his arm, and the faces of Tracy and Frazer were bleeding. Sam Blair stared incredulously across the counter at the Circle B men. Then he looked at Dan and Jack. A formidable fighting combination, he told himself. Before the fight started, he had been sure they were bound to lose.

The door of the store opened, and Horton walked in. He stared, open-mouthed at Dan and Jack, and the five men on the floor, then turned, and walked out.

Dan spoke to the Circle B men.

"I can see you've had enough," he said. "We'll send the doctor along. And tell Ballard it'll take more than a cowardly attack like this to get us out of the valley."

Dan and Jack left the store, had a few words with Horton outside, then walked over to see the doctor. Dan went in to tell Harper he was wanted in the store. Coming out, to rejoin Jack, he saw Mary Ballard riding into town. She stopped outside the store, and dismounted.

"I'll be back in a few minutes," said Dan to Jack, and walked over to Ballard's daughter. Once again, he was struck by her beauty, and he realized she had been in his thoughts frequently since their last meeting. She saw him approaching, recognized him, and waited, smiling, until he reached her.

"Mr Kilcane." she said. "Nice to meet you again. Sorry you left the ranch the other day before I had the chance to thank you properly."

She paused, as Doc Harper passed her with a brief greeting and went into the store.

"How is the ankle?" asked Dan.

"Nearly better," she replied. "It's healed up a lot quicker than the doctor figured. You haven't decided to move on yet, then?"

"No." replied Dan. "There's a job to do here that'll keep me occupied for a while."

"I'll probably see you around then," she said, glad that Dan was not leaving the valley just yet. She felt strongly attracted to him, and was experiencing a powerful desire to know him better. She turned towards the store, and stepped up on to the boardwalk.

"I wouldn't go in there just now," said Dan. "There's been a bit of a ruckus inside. Boyle's in there, with four Circle B hands. They're all a bit worse for wear. Doc Harper's taking a look at them now."

"They were brawling among themselves?" she asked.

"Not exactly," replied Dan. "They were trying to persuade a couple of strangers to leave the valley. And the way they were trying to persuade them was by beating them up."

Her dark eyes opened wide.

"I don't understand it," she said. "Who are the two strangers you're talking about?"

"One of them is myself," replied Dan, "and the other is my partner Jack

McLaren, standing over there, near the livery stable."

She looked in Jack's direction, then back at Dan.

"I can't believe what you're saying," she said. "Why should father want you and your friend to leave?"

Dan told her of all that had happened to the homesteaders, and to Jack and himself, since he had first arrived in the valley. He held nothing back.

"So," he went on, when he had finished, "me and my friend Jack are going to do our best to stop your father from turning the homesteaders off their land. I'm sorry, but it's something we feel we have to do."

"As a matter of fact," she said, "although I call him father, and use his name, he's actually my stepfather. Mother married twice. But he's always told me that when he needs the whole of the land in the valley for his cattle, the settlers will *have* to go. He says he'll offer them a fair price."

"Your father's wrong," said Dan.

"There's no question of the homesteaders *having* to leave. Their land belongs to them by right of settlement. Nobody has the right to turn them off it. If there was a decent lawman in the valley, he'd make sure that that didn't happen.

"All the homesteaders in the valley are set on staying," Dan went on. "What worries me now, is what your father's going to do next. Nobody's been killed yet, but that could easily change, if your father don't see reason."

She looked at him, doubt in her eyes.

"I can't believe father would be responsible for killing any of the settlers," she said, "but I'm going to have a long talk with him when I get back, about all the things you say he's been doing."

The door of the store opened and the doctor came out, followed by the five Circle B men. Boyle was holding his arm, and Tracy and Frazer had bandages on their heads. Barstow's face was badly bruised, and he was limping. Whitman, stooping slightly, and holding his stomach, glared venomously at Jack, standing outside the livery stable.

Mary Ballard watched, open-mouthed, as the five men climbed painfully on to their horses, and headed for the Circle B.

"You and your friend did *that*?" she asked. Dan nodded.

"What's father going to do when they get back to the ranch-house?" she asked.

"Don't expect he'll be too pleased to see them in that condition," replied Dan, "but I don't know what his reaction will be. We'll just have to try and be ready for anything he throws at us."

"I'm going into the store for a few minutes." she said, "then I'm going straight back to the ranch, to try and talk some sense into my father."

Some time later, when Mary was approaching the Circle B ranchhouse, she saw the five men who had attacked

Dan and Jack emerge, and walk over to the bunkhouse. Mary dismounted, and went inside the house. Her father was in the living-room. His face was black. He looked up as Mary came in.

"You've been talking with that man Kilcane," he said. "I don't want you to go anywhere near him. He's a troublemaker."

"He was telling me some things, father," she said, "which I didn't want to believe. Is it true that you stopped the doctor going to the homesteads, and set fire to one, and forced one family to leave the valley?"

"These are the sort of things that have to be done, if people are too obstinate to move," said Ballard. "I've got to have all the land here for my cattle."

"But it seems you have no right to turn the homesteaders off," she said. "The land is theirs."

Ballard's face hardened. He scowled at Mary.

"It's mine," he said. "I'm not

arguing. What I'm going to do is to get Kilcane and his friend out of the way, so I can talk to the homesteaders without any interference. I'll soon make them see reason."

"Just how are you going to get them out of the way?" she asked.

"No need for you to know about that," he replied, sharply. "And remember what I told you. Keep away from Kilcane."

He turned, and stomped out of the house.

Concerned, Mary looked after him. She had never been very close to her stepfather, and after her mother's death, he seemed to her to have become a harder, more ruthless man than before. She felt almost afraid of him at times, and now she was worried about his intentions towards Dan and his friend.

The following morning, Ballard rode into town, with four of his hands, and went to the Sheriff's Office. Seeing a note on the door saying the sheriff would be in around noon, they went into the saloon.

Half an hour later, the homesteader Horton, his wife beside him, drove his buckboard into town. Close behind him was a second buckboard carrying Frost, with his wife and daughter. As Horton passed the livery stable Dave Arnold ran out and stopped him.

"I've just come out of the saloon," he said. "Ballard's in there with four of his men. Seems like they're just waiting for the sheriff to come in to deputize the four hands, then Brand will ride out with them to arrest Kilcane and McLaren."

Horton thanked Arnold, then spoke urgently to Frost, who was waiting behind him. The two buckboards turned, and headed for the homesteads.

Just before one in the afternoon, Sheriff Brand rode on to the Rennie homestead with a sworn-in posse of four men, all Circle B hands. They rode up to the house. As they came to a stop about thirteen yards from the door, Dan and Jack stepped out, both carrying holstered guns, and stood facing the posse. Although Dan had not seen the four men accompanying Brand before, he knew they were Circle B men. They looked a hard-bitten quartet, thought Dan, picked more likely for their gun-handling ability than anything else.

The sheriff spoke to Dan and Jack.

"I'm taking you both in," he said. "These are properly sworn-in deputies with me. You'd better come quietly. The law's behind me in this."

"Seems to me the law in this valley's something of a joke," said Dan. "What's the charge?"

"Damage to property in the store, and disturbing the peace," replied Brand. "Let's go. You ain't got a chance against the five of us."

His hand, and those of his four deputies, moved close to the handles of their six-guns. Suddenly, there was a loud prolonged squeak from the direction of the barn, and turning their heads, the sheriff and his deputies saw that the big barn door, ten yards away, was gradually opening. When it had opened to its fullest extent, Rennie and Horton walked out, with ten other homesteaders all carrying rifles. They stood in a line, side by side, facing the posse.

"I've spoken to the storekeeper," said Horton, "and he told me that Ballard's men started the fight in the store, and that Boyle said Ballard would pay for any damage done. So I figure it's Boyle you want, sheriff, and the men who were with him. You'd better ride out to the Circle B."

Brand's face flushed, and his hand touched the handle of his six-gun. Then he looked at Dan and Jack, both poised, ready to spring into action. From them, his gaze passed on to the grim, tense faces of the homesteaders. He spoke to the deputies.

"Let's go," he said, hoarsely. He wheeled his horse, and followed by the others, he rode off the homestead.

Dan watched them leave, then spoke

to the homesteaders.

"I want to thank you men for coming along," he said. "If you hadn't been here, there might have been a shoot-out with the sheriff, which we don't really want. What we have to do now is to keep our guard up, and wait for Ballard's next move."

He waited, while Horton and the others got their horses from where they had been hidden behind the barn, and rode off towards their homesteads.

6

FOR the following six days, all was quiet on the homesteads, with no sign of Ballard's men. Almost an hour after midnight on the sixth day, Dan and Jack, both light sleepers, were wakened by the sound of distant gunfire, coming through the open door on the upper floor of the barn. They put their gun-belts on, and went to the barn door. Jack opened it, and they listened for a short while. The firing, almost continuous, appeared to be coming from the adjoining homestead to the north.

"Looks like Ballard's men are trying to get into Carver's house," said Dan. "There are two small children there. We'd better go and give Carver a hand."

Quickly, they shouted to tell Rennie where they were going, saddled their horses, and rode out to the track running just outside the homesteads, and parallel to their eastern boundaries. Turning north when they reached it, they rode as fast as they could in the dark, towards Carver's homestead. They could still hear firing ahead of them.

Just before the track reached Carver's boundary, it passed through a small grove of trees which had been cleared sufficiently to allow the passage of a buckboard. Jack and Dan, riding side by side, had no chance of seeing the strong, taut rope, tied at chest height to two trees, and crossing the track in front of them.

Both were swept cleanly out of their saddles, and over the backs of their mounts, to land painfully on the ground. Before they could recover and reach for their guns, two men ran from the shelter of the trees, held revolvers to their heads, and relieved them of their weapons. A third man, following hard on the heels of the others, tied their hands together, then went for their horses, which had stopped a little way along the track. Then he brought out the captors' horses from their hiding place in the grove. Dan and Jack, shaken but unhurt, were ordered to mount. The three men then mounted, and with two of them leading the horses of their captives, and the third riding behind, they headed south.

Dan had assumed that they were heading for the Circle B ranch-house, but after they had been riding for some time, he realized that they would have reached that destination a while back. They continued riding for another two hours, and just before sunrise, they stopped outside a small log shack, with a small corral close by.

Dan guessed that it was a line camp, on the Circle B boundary, for accommodating line riders, whose job it was to look after and contain the cattle. A line rider, in the winter months, could go for weeks without seeing anybody, and in those parts he could expect snowstorms and temperatures down to 30° below. From the direction followed during the ride, Dan guessed they were on the western boundary.

They all dismounted, and Dan and Jack, hands still tied, were taken into the cabin by two of the men. The third man put the horses in the corral, then followed the others inside. Looking round, Dan could see that the cabin was no more than a one-room shack, lacking even the meagre comforts of the average bunkhouse. It was quite light outside now, and for the first time Dan and Jack were able to get a good look at their captors. They were all strangers to both Dan and Jack.

One of them, who gave the impression of being the leader of the three, was a tallish, lean man, with a black stubble, a cold eye, and a sour expression. His name was Harker. The other two were called Robertson and Blair. Robertson was shorter than Harker, and stocky, with long black hair down to his shoulders. Blair was similar in build to Robertson, but when he took his hat off, the prisoners could see he was almost completely bald.

Harker told Dan and Jack to sit with their backs against the wall. When they had complied, Dan spoke to him.

"This is a fool thing you three are doing," he said. "Whatever you do to us, those homesteaders ain't going to quit."

"Don't know anything about that," said Harker. "Our orders were to bring you two here, and hold you till the boss decided what he was going to do with you. He said if you tried to get away, he didn't mind if we roughed you up some, so's you wouldn't think of trying it again. Just you remember that."

"You know you're breaking the law, don't you?" said Dan.

"Maybe so," said Harker, "but that don't scare us any, seeing as the lawman in this valley does exactly what Mr Ballard tells him to do."

The Circle B men checked the cabin, to make sure there were no firearms around. Then they checked the prisoners thoroughly for concealed weapons. After tying their captives' feet, and also tying their hands behind their backs, the three men left the cabin.

"Ballard sure fooled us," said Dan, as the door closed behind them. "I never figured he was up to setting a trap like that."

"I've got to agree," said Jack. "He's smarter than we thought. The problem is, how're we going to get ourselves out of the mess we've gotten into. I have a feeling that Ballard's already decided that he wants to put us out of the way, permanent, but maybe he ain't decided yet just how and when he's going to do it."

"I think you're right," said Dan. "We've got to get away from these three somehow, just as soon as we can."

Harker came in at that point, and they stopped talking. For the rest of the day there was at least one Circle B man in the cabin, guarding them, at any one time. Their hands were untied only at mealtimes, when all three men were present. It was clear that Ballard had impressed on his men the dire consequences to them of any successful escape attempt.

During the night, the three Circle B men stood guard inside the cabin in turn, and Jack and Dan, still bound, spent an uncomfortable night sleeping on the hard floor. They could see that there was no point in staying awake in the hope that an opportunity to escape might arise.

Around midday the following day, tied up inside the cabin, with Blair watching them, Dan and Jack heard voices outside. Shortly after, Harker came into the cabin with Ballard. Stony-faced, the rancher looked down at the two prisoners.

"I warned you not to stay on in the valley, Kilcane," he said.

"You've only yourself to blame," he went on, "for you and your friend ending up as prisoners here. You should have left when you had the chance."

"If you think them homesteaders are going to give in without a fight, just because we ain't with them, you're going to get a shock, Ballard," said Dan. "You're going to find that they're a lot tougher than you think.

"And something else you should be thinking about," Dan went on. "You big ranchers have had things your own way for far too long. Times are changing. The small ranchers and the homesteaders are going to have their fair share of public land, and the law is going to spread wide enough to stop ranchers like you from being too greedy, and from taking by force, land that already belongs to somebody else."

Ballard regarded Dan dispassionately. Then, abruptly, he turned and left the cabin, accompanied by Harker. They walked over to the corral fence, where Ballard's horse was tied.

"You did well, last night, catching those two," said the rancher to Harker. "Good work."

"How long d'you figure on keeping them here?" asked Harker.

"A couple more days, maybe," replied Ballard. "I've got some men driving some cattle into a small hollow south of here, on our south boundary. When they get them there, they'll alter a few brands with a running iron. When that's done, I'll send a man along here to tell you, and you can take Kilcane and McLaren along to that hollow, and we'll hang them for rustlers, and leave them strung up from one of the cottonwoods there.

"I'll tell the sheriff about it," he went on, "but he ain't going to give us any trouble. And when the homesteaders hear about Kilcane and his friend being dead, I figure they'll be a lot readier to listen to reason than they are now."

He paused for a moment, then continued:

"About four miles west of here," he said, "there's a small ravine, just inside our boundary. I came round that way this morning, to look at the cattle.

"Well," continued Ballard, "I found two dead cows in there. Wolves, for sure. Send Robertson and Blair out there, early tomorrow to see if they can hunt any down. They're both good rifle shots. Maybe they can find the den and take care of the she-wolf and the pups. But tell them to be back before nightfall. If they have no luck, we'll try some poison. You'll be all right here on your own till they get back?"

"Sure," replied Harker. "I'll take no chances with Kilcane and his partner."

Ballard left soon after, and nothing untoward occurred during the rest of that day and the following night. There was no relaxation of the vigilance of the guards. Blair and Robertson left the following morning, soon after breakfast, and Harker stayed in the cabin to guard Dan and Jack, who were sitting on the floor, with their backs against the wall.

Just after midday, Harker, in the middle of preparing a meal for himself and the prisoners, heard the sound of a horse just outside the cabin. He pulled his six-gun, went over to the window, and looked out. Then he ran to the door, opened it, and went outside, closing the door behind him.

Mary Ballard was standing by her horse, close to the corral fence. Surprise showing on his face, Harker walked over to her.

"Miss Ballard," he said. "What in tarnation are you doing out here?"

"I felt like a long ride this morning," she replied, "so I came out this way. I was just going to turn back a few miles north of here, and head for home, when my horse went lame. So I headed for this line camp, figuring I might get another mount here. It's the left hind foot that seems to be causing the trouble. Maybe you'd have a quick look at it."

"Sure," said Harker, and bent down to lift the foot. Mary, standing behind him, picked up from the ground a broken piece of the timber which had been used for the horizontal bars of the corral fence, and which she had earmarked, as she dismounted. She hesitated momentarily, then gritted her teeth, and struck Harker with the piece of timber, on the back of his head. The Circle B hand dropped the horse's leg, and slumped to the ground, face down.

Mary, shaking a little, placed Harker's arms on his back, and fastened his wrists together with his bandanna. Then she took his gun, and ran inside the cabin, and over to Dan and Jack.

"I've knocked Harker out," she said, as she rapidly undid the ropes around Dan's wrists, then did the same for Jack. Dan quickly untied the rope around his ankles, took the gun which Mary had brought in, and ran outside. Harker was sitting up, shaking his head. He cursed, as he saw Dan coming towards him. As Jack and Mary came out of the house, Dan went in for some rope. Bringing it outside, he bound Harker hand and foot, then he and Jack dragged the ranch-hand into the cabin, left him lying on the floor, and went out to rejoin Mary.

"Is Harker all right?" she asked. "I wasn't sure just how hard I should hit him."

"You got it just about right," said Dan. "He's got a sore head, but no permanent damage that I can see.

"We're sure glad that you took a hand in this, Miss Ballard," he went on, "because there was a strong chance that we'd both have been murdered in the next few days. But I'm wondering why you're going against your stepfather."

"Hadn't we better be leaving?" she asked, looking around, nervously. "I'll tell you later."

"The other two ain't coming back till sundown," said Dan. "I heard them say so before they left. We can take our time. First of all, meet my friend Jack McLaren."

After the introduction, Mary explained her presence there.

"I just happened to overhear father talking to the foreman Boyle yesterday vening, in the house." she said. "They didn't know I was listening. They were talking about you two being held in the line camp here, and father said he was going to frame you both for rustling, and then hang you. I could hardly believe my ears. He went on to say that two of the men here would be hunting wolves today, leaving one on guard.

"So I decided," she went on, "that I'd better ride out here this morning, and try to set you free."

"Lucky for us you did," said Jack.

"What d'you want to do now?" Dan asked her. "Your father will know you freed us, as soon as Harker is found."

"I'm not going back to the ranch-house," said Mary. "I can't live there any more. I know now that my stepfather's an evil man. And I'm frightened of him. I'd like to go with you two, wherever you're going."

"Sure," said Dan. "And I know exactly where that is. But first, let's collect all the provisions we can find

110

here. I figure there's plenty to last us for quite a while. And we'll take a few cooking utensils, and blankets for the three of us, and that axe I saw outside."

While looking around the outside of the cabin, Jack found the guns and gun-belts belonging to himself and Dan in a sack lying against the rear wall of the cabin. When they had collected into sacks the things they wanted to take with them, Dan and Jack saddled their own horses, which were in the corral, and rode off with Mary, in an easterly direction. They rode warily across the Circle B range, watching out for distant riders, but they reached the eastern boundary without seeing anybody, and rode along it for a while, before, with Dan in the lead, they turned and climbed up the slope out of the valley. Reaching the top, Dan led the way to the hollow he had explored a while ago, just after the homesteaders had asked for his help. From time to time Jack dismounted and walked back to obliterate their tracks at points where they had been unable to avoid leaving clear hoofprints.

They rode up to the large patch of brush which concealed the cabin, dismounted, pushed through it, and entered the cabin.

"This'll be our home for a while," said Dan. "If any Circle B riders come looking for us, this cabin is well hidden from anybody up on the rim of the hollow, and I figure it's unlikely that they'd ride down here. You won't mind staying here with us for a while, will you, Miss Ballard? It's the only reasonably safe hiding-place that I know of around here. I know it ain't quite what you're used to, but you can use the bed, and we can fix one of the blankets, to throw a curtain round it."

"This place is fine," she said. "I'll soon clean up the cabin."

"While you're doing that," said Dan, picking up the axe, "Jack and I'll make a clearing behind the cabin where we can put the horses when they ain't grazing out in the open."

It was getting dark by the time the two men had made the clearing, and had thrown some loose brush on to the cabin roof, to further conceal it from above. Dan led the horses into the clearing, and Jack got some wood for the stove and stacked it outside the door. Then he and Dan went inside, carrying the provisions and other items they had brought from the line camp, including Harker's six-gun and rifle. Mary had tidied up the inside of the cabin, and had swept the floor. Dan brought some wood in, and got the stove going, and they had a meal. When they had finished, Mary asked Dan what his future plans were for helping the settlers.

"We'll stay here for now," he said, "because your father's bound to scour the area, looking for you, as well as us. I think we're pretty safe here. We'll keep a watch for riders during the day, and go into the cabin if we see anybody heading this way.

"Now, about yourself," Dan went on. "We know you don't want to go back to the Circle B, and this ain't no fit place for you to stay any longer than you have to. Where d'you aim to live?"

"My mother's sister lives in Ellsworth, Kansas," said Mary. "She's a widow, and we always got on fine together. Maybe, later, I'd like to go to her. But first, I want to help you any way I can, to stop my stepfather from turning the settlers out of the valley."

"You sure about that?" asked Dan, admiring her spirit. "Things could get plenty dangerous around here."

"I'm sure," she said. "It makes my blood boil, to think of honest, hard-working people being turned off their own land, just because they haven't the strength to resist a greedy rancher. My stepfather's got to be stopped somehow, before any lives are lost."

"You're right there," said Dan. "The problem is, how to do it? Like I said,

I figure we'd best lie low here for the next few days, then I'll ride to Horton's place at night-time, and find out what's been going on in the valley. Then we can decide on our next move against Ballard."

7

THERE was no sign of Circle B riders the following day, but on the day after that, Jack, on watch near the rim of the hollow, saw two riders coming from the direction of the valley. He ran down to the cabin, to warn the others, and put the horses behind the cabin. Then all three watched from inside the brush.

The riders paused when they reached the rim of the hollow, and looked down into it for a few minutes. Then, seeing no sign of any human presence, they rode halfway round the rim, and disappeared from view. Jack climbed out of the hollow, and watched them until they were out of sight. Then he went back to the others.

"All clear," he said. "They headed west for a while, and then swung north."

"I'll ride in and see Horton tonight," said Dan. "It's time for us to find out what's happening in the valley."

Dan left after dark, riding down into the valley, then roughly parallel to the river, till he reached the boundary of Horton's homestead. He had seen or heard no one on the way. He headed towards the house, but dismounted well back from it, and continued on foot, taking what cover he could. His objective was to get close enough to the house to speak to Horton before being fired on. He stopped against a small shed, not far from the house.

"This is Kilcane," he shouted, then twice repeated himself.

There was silence for a short while, then Horton called out through the window. He could see a dim shape standing close to the hut.

"Come in with your hands up," he shouted. "I've got you covered."

Dan raised his hands, and walked towards the house. As he drew closer, he spoke to Horton again, and the homesteader was now sure that the voice he was hearing was Dan's. He went over to the door, let Dan in, and closed it behind him. His wife, Esther, lit a lamp standing on a small table.

"We sure are glad to see you," said Horton. "We guessed you were still alive when the sheriff and Ballard's men searched all the homesteads by force, but we figured it wouldn't take him long to find you, if you were still in the valley. Ballard's story was that they were chasing you because you'd been caught rustling cattle, which we all knew wasn't true. There's a story going around that Ballard's daughter has left him, and that she helped you to escape. Is that true?"

"It's true," replied Dan, and he went on to tell of how he and Jack had been captured, and of how they had escaped, with Mary's help. He told Horton that Mary was dead set against the way her stepfather was threatening the homesteaders, and that she had no intention of going back to live with him.

"Apart from having all your homesteads searched, has Ballard bothered you any?" asked Dan.

"No," replied Horton. "I guess he's too busy looking for you two and his daughter just now. But we're all expecting that he's going to start hassling us again before long."

"So long as Ballard's men are out searching for us," said Dan, "we'd better lie low. But as soon as it looks like he's going to start on you and the other homesteaders again, I want you to ride out to the hide-out, and let me know."

He went on to describe the exact location of the hide-out, and cautioned Horton not to pass the information on to anyone else, and to make sure he wasn't followed when he did ride out there. He also asked Horton not to tell anyone that Dan had been to see him. He felt sure that Horton would do as he asked.

"I'll be getting back there now," he said.

"You need any supplies?" asked Horton.

"We brought some from the line camp," said Dan, "but we'll need more soon. And we could do with some ammunition for our six-guns, and a rifle."

"I'll give you what I've got," said the homesteader. "I'll drive into town for replacements in the morning."

"Thanks," said Dan. "That'll be a big help to us."

He waited while Horton put some supplies and ammunition into a sack for him to take with him. Then he took his leave of the couple, and rode back to the hide-out, where he gave Mary and Jack the details of his conversation with Horton.

A week passed without incident before Dan, on lookout, just around sunset, saw Horton approaching the hollow. He stepped out from cover, waited as the homesteader rode up to him, and looked back searchingly along Horton's trail. There was no sign of anyone following him. He greeted the homesteader, and led him down to the cabin. They went inside, and sat down with Jack and Mary.

"You've sure got yourself a good hide-out," commented Horton. "How did you find it?"

"I rode out looking for a place, just after you asked me to help you," said Dan. "I figured it might come in useful. You got some news for us?"

"I have," replied Horton. "Four days after you came to my place, four men rode into town, on their way to the Circle B. I was just coming out of the store, when I saw them ride in, and stop outside the saloon. They were all about the same height, a little on the tall side, and one of them was clearly the leader. His face looked like it was carved in stone, and there was a hard, bleak look in his eye. He was riding a big black horse — a fine animal.

"He looked across at me," Horton

went on, "then up and down the street, and I got the feeling that during that one short look, he had registered everything of importance to him. He was wearing a right-hand six-gun, and there was a rifle in his saddle holster. The three men with him were all armed in the same way, and they looked pretty near as mean as their leader. One of them was a half-breed.

"What struck me as odd," continued Horton, "was that they all wore the same sort of clothes, like it was a uniform, almost. And they were all dressed in black."

"They sound like professional gun-fighters," said Jack. "What did they do in town?"

"They went into the saloon," replied Horton, "and enquired the way to the Circle B ranch-house. After a drink, three of them left. The fourth stayed drinking for a while, and left later."

"Looks like Ballard's sent for some help to clear the settlers out," said Dan.

"I reckon you're right," said Horton, "and I can tell you who they are. Dave Arnold saw them about a year ago, when he was in a saloon in Denver, Colorado. Seems that somebody once called them the Liquidators, and the name stuck. The leader is called Marlin. The half-breed is called Morgan, and the other two are Drummond and Hill. Hill's the one who stayed on in the saloon for a while, the day the four men turned up in Lorimer. Arnold heard in Denver that Hill certainly liked his liquor, and he spent a lot of time on his own in a saloon there. Liquor didn't fuddle him, just made him a lot meaner, and the story was that Marlin put up with his drinking habits, because they were related in some way, and because Hill was a first-rate gunfighter, and reliable when the time for action came, whether he had a few drinks inside him, or not.

"According to Arnold," Horton went on, "they said in Denver that if anybody with the right kind of money wants a dirty job doing, and the Liquidators agree to take it on, they'll guarantee a satisfactory result."

"Have they made a move yet?" asked Dan.

"I was just coming to that," replied Horton. "Yesterday, that's two days after I saw Marlin and the others ride into town, I drove my buckboard into Lorimer. Esther was with me, and the Carvers were right behind me, on their own buckboard. We all went into the store. After a while, Carver and I came out, to go over to the bank, leaving the others behind.

"When we left the store," Horton went on, "Marlin and the other three were standing in the street outside, waiting for us. I can tell you, for a minute there, I was half-expecting them to blast us down. But Marlin wanted to talk. He asked me if my name was Horton, and when I said it was, he asked me to pass a message to all the homesteaders.

"Marlin said," Horton continued,

"that we all had exactly one week from that day, to pack up, and leave the valley. He said he was relying on me and Esther to show a good example to all the other settlers, and he was going to pay me a visit in a week's time, to see if we'd quit. If we hadn't, he and his men were going to set fire to my buildings, and then run me and Esther out of the valley. And if we tried to come back, we'd be killed.

"Marlin told me," Horton went on, "that there was no use the homesteaders trying to get together to fight Ballard. He said that they wouldn't stand a chance against his own men and Ballard's men put together. Then he and his men rode off. The way he spoke to me, with that gravelly voice of his, and with that cold look in his eye, I could tell he was deadly serious."

"You've told the other homesteaders what Marlin said?" asked Jack.

"Yes," replied Horton. "I've been round them all, and there's no doubt they're a mite worried about Marlin's threat, some more than others, especially since they don't know that you and your friend are still alive. But up to now, nobody's taken a decision to leave."

"When you get back, you can tell them that Jack and I are alive and free," said Dan, "but don't tell them where we're hiding out. Seems like we've got to think up some way of stopping Marlin from doing what he's threatened to do to you six days from now. And it ain't going to be easy. You'd better ride back now. If we have to get in touch with you, one of us will ride to your place. Tell the others we're going to do our best to help them."

When Horton had departed, Jack spoke to Dan and Mary.

"You got any ideas?" he asked. "Looks like we've got a tough job on our hands."

"I've got the germ of an idea sitting right in the back of my mind," said Dan, "but it needs to grow a bit before we can talk about it."

"It all seems rather hopeless," said Mary. "Nobody could really blame you both if you just rode right out of the valley."

"That's not the way I see it," said Dan. "What Ballard's doing is wrong, and he's got to be stopped. And don't forget he took us both prisoner. It's personal now."

Jack nodded agreement.

"What we've got to do," said Dan, "is to give Ballard something else to think about, apart from getting rid of the homesteaders, and I've just this minute had an idea about that."

He went on to explain what he had in mind.

"It'll mean though," he said to Mary, when he had finished, "that Dan and I'll have to set off early, and you'll be here on your own all day."

"I'm going with you," she said. "I'll be a lot happier with you than hiding here. And I know the Circle B range very well. Mother and I used to take some long rides together, three or four

127

times a week when the weather was good."

"All right," said Dan. "I reckon you can help us a lot. What we're looking for is a big depression, with steep walls and water and grazing, somewhere close to the boundary. It's got to have only one entrance, and it's got to be somewhere where there ain't much chance of Circle B riders passing by."

Mary thought long and hard. Then she spoke.

"I know just the place," she said. "It's near the south-east corner of the range, and not all that far from here. Mother and I came across it one day, and had a picnic there. I'm sure I can find it again, without too much trouble."

"Right," said Dan, "we'll head south from here, then we don't need to ride on to Circle B range until we're close to the place you're talking about. You sure you ain't got no regrets about going against your stepfather like this?"

"None at all," she replied. "What he's doing is wrong, very wrong. That's why I'm going to help you to stop him. And since we're working together, we really should be using first names, don't you think?"

The two men nodded.

They left the following morning, an hour before sunrise, and reached the depression when the sun was already quite high in the sky. They had seen no Circle B riders down in the valley while on their way. All three rode down into the depression, and looked around.

"This is perfect," said Dan. "We can start bringing the cows in right away."

They rode out of the depression, and looked north across the range. Grazing cattle were scattered over the valley floor.

"We'll gather around twenty cows each," said Dan. "You up to this, Mary?"

"Sure," she replied. "I should be, considering the number of times I rode out with mother to watch the round-ups, and saw the hands at work."

The three fanned out, and headed for the distant cows. Each of them collected twenty head, and drove them into the depression. Mary more than held her own during this operation. When they had finished, they stretched a rope across the narrow trail leading into the depression, to prevent the cows from leaving. During the operation, they had seen no signs of Circle B riders.

"So far, so good," said Dan. "What we have to do now is to make sure that somebody finds these cattle pretty soon. Like I said yesterday, it's bound to take Ballard's mind off the homesteaders some, if he thinks there are rustlers around.

"When I was collecting those cows," he went on, "I had a look in that small box canyon over there." He pointed. "It's only two hundred yards away, and there's a patch of brush inside. I reckon if we got that brush burning well, somebody'd be bound to see the smoke cloud, and ride out here to investigate. And from the entrance to that canyon, they'd be able to look down into this basin, and see the cows we've collected. It won't take them long to find the rope, and from then on, I'm hoping they'll be convinced that rustlers are at work."

They rode to the box canyon, and started the fire at several points. They could see that there was no danger of the fire spreading beyond the confines of the canyon itself. They waited until the brush was well alight, then returned quickly to the entrance to the depression in which the cattle were being held. Jack then led the way south, out of the valley, leaving clear tracks, but when they reached a point on hard ground well south of the boundary of the Circle B range, he swung east, then north, making sure that they were making no visible tracks for anyone to follow. As they headed for their hide-out, they looked across towards the valley. They could see the smoke, rising high into the sky.

The following morning Dan, with Mary and Jack, walked over to the pit which Dan had found on his first visit to the hollow.

"I've got a notion that we might be able to use this," he said, "but first, I want to have a good look inside it, with a lamp."

As he had done once before, he tied a rope round the boulder close to the pit entrance, then climbed down it into the pit. Jack followed him, and Mary lowered a lighted lamp down to them. With this, they examined the interior of the pit closely. Then they climbed out.

"Couldn't be better," said Dan, and explained to the others what he planned to use the pit for.

"Tomorrow evening we'll ride into Lorimer, Jack," he went on. "Maybe we'll strike it lucky. Maybe what we want will be there then."

He turned to Mary.

"I'm sorry we'll have to leave you, Mary," he said, "but it's a two-handed job we have to do. And you'll be safer here. Will you be all right?"

"I'll be fine," she replied.

The two men left not long before sunset the following day. When they reached Lorimer, they rode along the backs of the houses on the main street, until they came to the livery stable. They tied their horses behind the stable, out of sight of the street, and walked over to the house occupied by the livery stable owner. The door was opened by Arnold. His eyes widened as he recognized them, and he quickly ushered them inside.

"I heard from Horton you were both all right," he said. "For a while, we thought we'd never see you again."

"It nearly came to that," said Dan, "but we had a stroke of luck.

"Have you heard any news from the Circle B today?" he went on.

"Two of the hands were in town late this afternoon," replied Arnold, "and the saloon keeper Herb Turner overheard them talking about some cattle thieves operating on the south boundary. It seems that Ballard was in a real rage, and he'd sent most of his men out across the south boundary to look for the rustlers. The men said something about the rustlers having started a range fire by accident, which forced them to run off before they were caught."

"That's very interesting," said Dan. "And now there's some more information you might be able to give us. We're interested in one of Marlin's men called Hill. I guess you know him."

"Sure do," said Arnold. "I first saw him in Denver. He's the one with the long, narrow face, and the drooping moustache. All four of them are killers, but I did hear that Marlin and Hill seemed to find even more pleasure than the others in gunning people down."

"I've heard," said Dan, "that Hill is

fond of his liquor, and he sometimes drinks alone."

"That's right," said Arnold. "The other three never have more than one drink at a time. Maybe they figure that any more would slow their gun hands down."

"I expect that Hill's been visiting the saloon here, then," said Dan.

"Yes," replied Arnold. "He was in there yesterday evening for a couple of hours, sitting alone at a table, with a bottle and a glass. Herb Turner don't like him in there, though he sure ain't going to tell him that to his face. Herb says it ain't good for business. Hill throws a sort of gloom over the place.

"And I saw him go in again about an hour ago, on his own," Arnold went on. "I expect he's still there."

Arnold walked over to a window and looked out.

"Yes, he's still there," he said. "I can see his horse outside the saloon, standing under the light. It's a big chestnut. If he stays as long as he did yesterday evening, he'll be there for another hour or so."

Before they left Arnold, Dan handed him some money and a list, and asked him if he would buy some provisions for them at the store, and get them out to Horton's place. Dan asked him to tell Horton that Dan would pick up the provisions during the next few days.

On leaving Arnold, Dan and Jack walked along the backs of the houses until the buildings petered out, except for one solitary, unoccupied shack, about a hundred yards further on. The trail from town to the Circle B ranch-house passed in front of this shack, then veered sharply to the left.

The two men walked on to the shack, and stood against it, looking back towards town. They could see the big light outside the saloon, and Hill's chestnut standing underneath it. While they were watching, two men rode in from the other side of town and went into the saloon. Then one man walked out and went over to the store. Then, forty five minutes after they had started their watch, they saw Hill come out of the saloon, mount the chestnut, and canter down the street towards them. They moved around to the side of the shack, out of Hill's view, and Jack prepared to use the lariat he was carrying.

He grasped the main line and the broad loop in his throwing hand, and in the other he held the coils containing the remainder of the rope. Just after Hill passed the shack, Jack stepped out, and in the dim light, he made an overhand toss for Hill's head. The rope dropped neatly over Hill's shoulders, and Jack jerked the loop tight to pinion Hill's arms while he heaved him out of the saddle.

Moving fast, Dan was at the fallen man's side as soon as he hit the ground. He relieved him of his gun, and with Jack's help, he bound Hill's hands together, and gagged him. Then he stood by the prisoner, while Jack went to bring back the horse, which had run on for a short distance.

When Jack returned, he left the animal with Dan, and went back to the livery stable to collect their horses. When he rejoined Dan, they hoisted Hill into the saddle. Then, with Dan leading Hill's horse, they rode back to the hide-out, following a route over which tracking, for the most part, would be impossible.

Lying awake in the cabin, Mary heard Dan calling. Looking out of the window, she could see that dawn was not far away. She went out into the open, and saw three riders approaching. She recognized Dan and Jack as the riders on two of the horses. They stopped in front of her.

"I sure am glad to see you back," she said, then looked at the third rider. She could see that his hands were bound, and that he was gagged.

"Who's that?" she asked. "Our first prisoner?"

"Our first prisoner," agreed Dan.

138

"One of the notorious Liquidators. Name of Hill. Let's get him inside, and have a good look at him."

Mary went into the cabin to light the lamp, while Jack and Dan pulled Hill down from his horse, removed the gag, and directed him into the cabin, where he was ordered to sit down on the floor, with his back against the wall.

The prisoner stared in turn at the other three occupants of the cabin. His eyes were blazing, and his long narrow face was twisted with rage.

"You must be mad," he said, harshly. "You're all as good as dead. I figure you must know who I am."

"We know who you are, all right," said Dan. "One of Marlin's killers. That's why you're here."

"It won't take Marlin and the others long to find you," said Hill, "and when he does you'll all be very sorry you brought me out here like this. You must be the two men Ballard told us about. And you," he went on, looking at Mary, "must be Ballard's daughter."

"You've guessed right," said Dan. "But if I were you, Hill, I wouldn't be too sure that Marlin's going to find you. You'll be too well hidden for that."

He looked out of the window.

"I think it's light enough now," he went on, "for us to introduce you to your new home. But first, Jack, just loosen that rope around his wrists a little, so that he'll be able to work it loose, and free his own hands after a while."

Jack told Hill to stand up, then he did what Dan had requested. Then all four of them walked over to the pit which Dan and Jack had explored recently. Dan tied two lariats together, as Hill stared, fascinated and with mounting apprehension, first at the rope, then at the mouth of the pit.

"You're crazy if you think I'm going down there," he said, then froze as Jack grabbed his arm in a vice-like grip, and jammed the muzzle of his six-gun against the prisoner's head.

"You're going down," said Jack, grimly, "and if you don't go quiet, I'll lay the barrel of my sidearm along your head, and we'll just drop you in there.

"And when you're down there," Jack went on, "maybe you'll begin to realize that we're doing you a big favour. Maybe we can kill that bad drinking habit of yours."

Hill, seething with rage, stood still while Dan coiled the middle of the long length of rope he was holding, several times around Hill's body, under the arms. Then Jack and Dan, each holding a length of rope, pushed Hill into the mouth of the pit and lowered him towards the floor. Hill cursed as he disappeared from sight. When the weight went off the ropes, Jack released his end, and Dan pulled the coils free from Hill's body, and lifted the complete rope out of the pit. Then Dan and Jack leaned over the pit mouth. They could hear Hill still cursing vigorously. He stopped, as Dan shouted down to him.

"You'll find you've got all the comforts of home down there," said Dan. "Nice fresh water running through. Some food in a sack. Blankets, and a lamp and some coal oil, in case you get scared in the night. And you can even have a fire down there, if you want. We'll drop some firewood down for you, later on. What else could you wish for, except, maybe, a bar?"

The sound of Hill's renewed outburst of cursing faded as they walked back to the cabin.

"That's an evil man," said Mary. "I suppose there's no chance of him escaping from that pit?"

"Not on his own," replied Dan. "It would be impossible."

Jack nodded in agreement.

"What's our next move?" asked Mary.

"Something else to take your step-father's mind off the homesteaders,

I think," replied Dan. "I'm going to see if I can work something out. Meanwhile, we'd better carry on watching for riders coming this way."

8

SHORTLY after the time when Hill had been consigned to the pit, Marlin knocked on the door of the Circle B ranch-house. It was opened by Ballard.

"I'm riding into town," said Marlin. "Hill didn't come back last night. His bunk ain't been slept in."

"Maybe he's sleeping it off in town, somewhere," said Ballard. "He sure does like his liquor."

"Hill never gets drunk," said Marlin, sharply. "I'll ride into town, and see what's happened to him. Have your men picked up those rustlers yet?"

"Not yet," replied Ballard. "They followed their tracks across the south boundary, but lost them soon after. They're riding further south, to see if they can pick them up again. We don't know for certain yet, whether they've actually driven any Circle B cows out of the valley."

Marlin returned later in the morning. He rode up to Ballard, who was talking to his foreman, Boyle, and dismounted. He spoke to Ballard.

"Hill has disappeared," he said. "He left the saloon after dark to ride back here, and just went missing. There's no sign of him or his horse on the trail between here and town. You figure he might have been ambushed by those two that your men let go. Kilcane and McLaren, wasn't it?"

Ballard flushed.

"Maybe," he replied. "But ain't it unlikely that a gunfighter of Hill's class would let them get the better of him?"

"The fact is, he's missing," said Marlin, "and we've got to find him. He's a cousin of mine, and the best shot in the gang, with rifle or revolver. It beats me, what can have happened to him. I suppose you ain't got no idea of where Kilcane and McLaren and

145

that daughter of yours might be? It's beginning to look as if they might have Hill. Or maybe they've killed him."

"If I knew where they were, I'd have picked them all up before now," said the rancher. "I think it's time that we searched all the homesteads again. Maybe your cousin is on one of them, with Kilcane and McLaren. I've still got four hands here, who didn't go out after the rustlers. I'll get the sheriff to go round with them, to search the homesteads, in case some of them settlers ain't too keen on co-operating."

"I'll go along with them," said Marlin, "and if I get the idea that any of them's hiding anything, I'll get Morgan and Drummond to pay them a special visit tonight, to persuade them to talk. It's something they're pretty good at."

"If nothing turns up at the homesteads," said Ballard, "I'll mount a full-scale search of the valley for Hill, and the three we're after, as soon as my hands get back from chasing those rustlers."

Marlin joined four of Ballard's men who were waiting for him, and all five headed for town. They picked up the sheriff, then rode across the ford, and turned towards the line of ten homesteads north of town, to start their search.

★ ★ ★

At the hide-out, on the same day, Dan and Jack rested for a time, then had a meal, while Mary kept watch. Earlier, Dan had thrown down some firewood and matches to the prisoner. When Jack relieved Mary at the look-out position, she came to help Dan collect some wood for the stove. Then they sat down inside the cabin.

"I've been thinking hard about our next move," said Mary, "and I've come up with an idea I'd like you to listen to."

Dan smiled at her. "Fire away," he said.

"Well," she said, "on part of the

west range, so that he could use it for raising cattle, my stepfather had to locate underground water in two places, and had to use windmills to pump the water up for the cattle. I figure that if those two windmills could be put out of action for a while, it would give him something extra to think about."

Dan looked at Mary, admiringly.

"There you go," he said. "For three or four hours I've been racking my brains, and I ain't come up with anything half so good as what you've just suggested.

"It so happens," he went on, "that I've helped put up a few windmills in my time, and I know just the way to put one out of action for a spell."

"The cattle wouldn't come to any harm, would they?" asked Mary.

"Not if Ballard did the right thing," replied Dan. "A cattle breeder once told me that a cow could drink up to thirty gallons of water a day, so those cattle relying on the windmills for water would have to be moved to other parts of the range, where there was enough water and grazing for them, as well as for the cows that were already there.

"This is a job for one man," Dan went on. "There'll be less chance of being seen. Ballard may have men out searching the range, so it'll have to be done at night. Can you tell me exactly where I'll find those two windmills?"

"They ain't all that far from that line camp you were held in," she replied, and went on to describe their exact location.

"I'll leave just before dark," said Dan. "Good thing there's a moon tonight. I should be able to spot those windmills well before I reach them. I should be back before dawn. I'll take an oil lamp with me, for when I climb up the towers to put the windmills out of action. Not much chance of anybody seeing it."

"You sure you don't want Jack to go along with you?" she asked.

"No," Dan replied. "He's needed

here, to keep an eye on you and the prisoner. I'll go now, and tell him what I plan to do."

Dan left later, just before sunset. The sky was clear, as he rode out of the hollow, and headed towards the valley.

Mary slept only fitfully that night, and before dawn, she rose, with the intention of going to the lookout point to await Dan's arrival. When Jack heard her moving, he got up himself, and accompanied her. They stood in silence for a while, looking towards the west, the direction from which they expected Dan to come. Then Mary spoke.

"I'm worried," she said. "When I suggested cutting off those water supplies, I never thought Dan would go alone. I'm praying he'll get back safe."

"To go alone was the right thing to do," said Jack. "And myself, I ain't worried about him not getting back. I know him too well."

"I heard you served in the Cavalry together," said Mary.

"Yes," said Jack. "Dan was my lieutenant. He was a fine horse soldier, always thinking of his men. Twice he saved my life. Once, when we . . . "

He broke off, and looked towards the west.

"There's a horse coming this way," he said. "Stay quiet."

They stood listening, as the sound of a walking horse grew louder. Then, faintly, the whistled rendition of The Yellow Rose of Texas floated to their ears, and they saw the dim outline of a man on horseback approaching.

"That's Dan," said Jack. "That's his favourite tune."

Mary breathed a sigh of relief.

Jack called out, and Dan came to a stop in front of them, and dismounted.

"It's been a long ride," he said, "and I'm some tuckered out, but the job's done. Those two windmills are going to be out of action for quite a while. I guess I'll take a few hours' sleep now, while I've got the chance."

"Right," said Jack. "As soon as it's light, I'll come back here on lookout. I figure that Ballard's men, and Marlin's too, will soon be combing the area for us and Hill, and there's a chance that some of them might ride this way."

"You're right," said Dan, "and I think we should make ourselves a bit harder to spot. We could pile some more brushwood around the cabin, and up on the roof, and we could roll some biggish rocks around the mouth of the pit. If they don't see anything interesting in the hollow there, maybe they won't bother to ride down."

"If Mary'll keep a lookout, I'll do all that while you're resting," said Jack. "The sooner it's done, the better."

"I'll come up here as soon as it's light," said Mary.

When Dan came out of the cabin three hours later Jack had completed the screening of the cabin, and the mouth of the pit, and Mary was still on lookout

"How's the prisoner?" asked Dan.

"He's still spouting a lot of bad language down there," replied Jack, "but his appetite's all right. He seems to be eating everything I drop down there."

"Bit of a comedown for him," said Dan. "One minute, he's a notorious gunfighter, and a member of the Liquidators, whose name sends a shiver down most folks' backs, and who always reckon to get their man. And the next minute, he's a prisoner, stuck in a hole in the ground, without a gun, and with no company but his own. It must be quite an experience for him."

"Reckon so," said Jack. "I've been wondering," he went on, "what's happening in the valley just now."

"There's bound to be a big search on for us," said Dan. "By now, they'll be suspecting we had something to do with Hill disappearing, and maybe they're beginning to wonder whether there *are* any rustlers after all. And if they haven't done so already, they'll soon find those two damaged windmills, and put that down to us as well."

"I think," Dan went on, "that we'd better ride over to see Horton after dark, to find out just what's happening in the valley. And we can pick up those provisions I asked Arnold to buy for us and pass on to Horton. I reckon we should both go, in case we run into trouble, and Mary should come as well. I don't like the idea of leaving her here on her own, with things like they are now."

Dan walked out of the hollow to relieve Mary, and he told her about the proposed visit to Horton.

"I'm glad to be going along," she said, "but is it safe to leave Hill here on his own?"

"Don't see what harm he can do," replied Dan.

"There's no way he can get himself out of that pit."

★ ★ ★

At about the time Dan and Mary were speaking, the sheriff, accompanied by Marlin and four Circle B hands, rode up to the Horton homestead and, brushing Horton's objections aside, they searched the house and buildings. The sheriff, with Marlin by his side, asked Horton if he knew where Dan and Jack were hiding out.

"I don't," replied Horton. "What d'you want them for?"

"We've got clear evidence they've been rustling cattle," said the sheriff.

"Even if I knew where they were, I wouldn't tell you," said Horton. "They ain't rustlers, and you know it. Any evidence you've got must be faked."

"You'd better mind what you're saying, Horton," said the sheriff angrily. Abruptly, he mounted his horse and rode off.

Marlin stayed behind for a moment, to speak to Horton.

"Don't forget what I told you the other day," he said. "If you ain't out of the valley three days from now, you're in real trouble."

Leaving Horton, Marlin caught up with the sheriff.

"Horton's lying," he said. "I'm sure of it. You say he's the leader of the homesteaders?"

The sheriff nodded. "Yes," he said, "and I reckon you're right about him lying."

That evening, just before midnight, Drummond and Morgan rode on to the Horton homestead, left their horses well back from the house, and approached it on foot. Moving carefully, they avoided the alarm trip wires, about which they had been warned, and stood against the door of the house. Drummond tapped lightly on the door.

Inside the house, Horton and his wife were in bed. Since Marlin's ultimatum had been given, they had felt reasonably sure that they were safe from attack until the week which he had given them had expired. Horton, not yet asleep, heard the tapping, got out of bed, lit the lamp in the living-room, and went to the door.

"Who's there?" he called.

Drummond answered in a low voice. "It's Kilcane," he said.

Horton, who had been expecting Dan to call for the provisions Arnold had bought for him, withdrew the stout bar which was securing the door, and started to pull the door open. Drummond threw his whole weight against it, and it smashed against Horton's forehead and the upper part of his body, and sent him reeling across the room, to fall on the floor, temporarily dazed. Drummond and Morgan walked into the living-room, closed the door behind them, and stood watching the homesteader, their six-guns in their hands. Horton's wife, wakened by the noise, came running into the room, stared at the two intruders, then went to kneel by her husband, who was attempting to rise.

Drummond grabbed Horton by the arm, lifted him up, tied his hands

157

together behind him, and sat him down on a nearby chair. Morgan gestured to Horton's wife, and she sat down on a chair a few feet away from her husband.

Drummond waited until Horton appeared fully conscious, then he spoke to the homesteader.

"When Marlin was here earlier today," he said, "he was sure you were lying when you said you didn't know where Kilcane and his friend are hiding out. After all, you're the leader of the settlers here. We figure you're bound to know. So we've come along to get the information from you."

"I can't tell you what I don't know," said Horton.

Drummond scowled at him, and shook his head.

"You're a fool, Horton," he said. "We're bound to get the information out of you in the end. Especially if my friend here starts work on you."

He pointed to the half-breed, Morgan,

who was watching them, a six-gun in his hand.

"He's a bit of a specialist on Indian tortures," Drummond went on. "But maybe I can manage without him."

He walked up to Horton, and slapped him with all his strength, first on one cheek, then the other. Horton's head jerked from side to side, as the blows hit, then a trickle of blood ran down his right cheek. Esther Horton started to rise, to go to him, but Morgan roughly forced her back into her chair.

"The hide-out, Horton," said Drummond. "Where is it?"

"Don't know," mumbled Horton, still dazed from the blows.

Drummond repeated the two blows, one to each cheek, and the home-steader's left cheek started to bleed. Then Drummond, a big, powerful man, yanked Horton to his feet with his left hand, hit him hard in the stomach with his right fist, and pushed him down on to the chair again.

"The hide-out?" asked Drummond.

Horton, doubled up, and unable to speak, slowly shook his head from side to side.

"You're a stubborn man, Horton," said Drummond. "Maybe we'd better try another tack."

He told Morgan to tie the woman's hands behind her, and when his partner had done this, he walked over to stand in front of the homesteader's wife, and spoke to Horton again.

"This is a fine-looking woman you've got, Horton," he said. "A pity to spoil those good looks. But that's what I'm going to have to do, if you don't tell us what we want to know."

He raised his right fist.

"No!" shouted Horton, "damn you." Handicapped as he was by his bound hands, he rose from his chair, and rushed at Drummond with the intention of forcing him away from his wife. Drummond quickly sidestepped, and as Horton blundered past him, he struck the homesteader savagely, on the back of his head with the barrel of his gun.

Horton went down as if poleaxed, and his head slammed hard against the floor. There was a loud, despairing cry from his wife. As she tried to rise, she was once again forced back in her chair by Morgan. Drummond waited for Horton to come round, but when the homesteader showed no signs of movement, he holstered his gun, and knelt down beside him. He bent over Horton for a while. Then he looked up at Morgan, frustration in his face.

"He's gone and died on us," he said, rising to his feet.

Horton's wife screamed suddenly, and eluding Morgan's grasp, she ran to her husband, and knelt down beside him. Ignoring her, Drummond turned to speak to Morgan.

"We'd better . . . " he said, breaking off as the door suddenly burst open, and Dan ran in, closely followed by Jack. Seeing a gun in Morgan's hand, Dan put a bullet in the half-breed's right forearm, and the gun fell to the floor. Dan then held his gun on Morgan.

Jack, reaching Drummond before the latter had his gun out, dazed him with a crushing right-hand blow to the side of the head, then, exerting all his considerable strength, and seemingly without effort, he hurled him against the wall of the room and took his gun as he lay, moving feebly, on the floor.

"Watch them both, Jack," said Dan, and went quickly over to Horton and his wife, who was cradling the homesteader's head in her arms. She was sobbing. Dan knelt down beside her, and checked Horton's pulse. Slowly, he shook his head.

"I'm sorry," he said to Esther Horton. "He's gone. Was it Drummond?" She nodded.

Dan went to the door, and called Mary in. She went over to the sobbing woman, and knelt down beside her. Dan turned to look at Morgan and Drummond. His face was grim. Morgan was holding his wounded forearm. Drummond, who had lifted himself a little to sit against the wall, was glaring up at Jack. His face was badly bruised, both from contact with Jack's fist, and his collision with the wall.

"These men have got to be dealt with by the law, Jack," said Dan, "but not by the kind of law we've got in the valley just now. We'll have to wait till we can hand them over to a proper lawman. Maybe we can get a Deputy U.S. Marshal here later on. Meantime, we've got to fasten them away where they can do no more harm. We'll take them back with us.

"Jack," he went on. "Hitch up that buckboard I saw outside, then we can take Mrs Horton and her husband along to the Rennie homestead. I know they're good friends. They'll look after her for the time being."

"Those provisions," said Esther Horton, suddenly, pointing to a large sack in the corner of the room. "They're for you."

"Thanks," said Dan. "We're going to need them. You fit to ride along to the Rennies now?" She nodded her head.

Dan went to look at the wound on Morgan's forearm. It was a deep graze, but the bone had not been touched.

"It'll keep," said Dan, then he and Jack tied their prisoners' hands behind them, before Jack went to get the buckboard ready. When he brought it up to the door of the house, he lifted Horton's body into it. Mrs Horton climbed up to the seat.

"I'll drive it," she said.

Dan and Jack hoisted the prisoners on to their horses. Then they all set off for the Rennie homestead, Dan, with Mary beside him, riding in front, leading the prisoners' horses, and Jack bringing up the rear.

When they reached their destination, Dan told Rennie and his wife what had happened, and Martha Rennie took Horton's widow inside.

"We'll look after Esther," said Rennie. "And we'll see to the burying. Where are you taking these two men?"

"I figure it's best to keep that dark just now," said Dan, "but you can take it from me, they'll be somewhere where they can't do no more harm for the time being. I'm hoping that now Marlin's lost his three men, Ballard will maybe leave you homesteaders alone for a while."

"I sure hope so," said Rennie. "Can we get in touch with you, if we want you?"

"I don't figure it's safe for you to ride out to our hide-out," replied Dan. "Jack or I'll ride out to your place if we want to talk. In the meantime, I'd appreciate it if you'd get some more provisions for us from the store. We've got some more mouths to feed from now on. We'll collect them from you when we can."

He told Rennie what he wanted, and handed some money over. Then a thought struck him.

"It would be Marlin who sent his two men to Horton's place," he said, "and he's bound to start looking for them, as well as Hill, when they don't turn up at the ranch. I reckon it might be a good idea for you to put around the story in town, as early in the morning as you can, that Horton's wife found him last evening, beaten up and dead, not far from his house, and she'd no idea who'd done it. That should keep her from harm, and it'll sure make Marlin scratch his head.

"Don't you worry," he went on, "and tell the others not to. I figure we'll win in the end."

Shortly after, Dan, Jack and Mary left with the two prisoners. During the ride, Drummond cursed and threatened intermittently. Morgan remained stoically silent.

When they reached the hide-out, after a long, slow ride, they stopped close to the pit entrance. Dan dismounted, and looked inside. The interior was in darkness. He shouted down to Hill to light the lamp, and shortly after, he saw the dim light inside the pit, just as Mary brought a lighted lamp from the cabin, and stood it on the ground near him.

"We've got two friends of yours here, Hill," shouted Dan. "They'll be coming down to see you shortly. Stand well back, or you'll get a bullet through you."

Jack and Dan pulled Morgan and Drummond from their horses, and pushed them up to the pit mouth, where, using a long length of rope, they lowered them into the pit, one after the other, in the same way as they had recently lowered their partner, Hill. They heard, coming from below, the sound of conversation, liberally sprinkled with curses, as Hill untied the ropes binding the hands of Morgan and Drummond.

"Have we any bandaging, Mary?" Dan asked.

"For Morgan?" she asked. Dan nodded.

"I'll get some from the cabin," she said.

"Right," said Dan. "I'll drop it down for him. There's plenty of water down there for him to wash the wound. And later on, I'll drop some food down. Meanwhile, we'd better get some rest."

9

MARLON was in a foul mood as he rode up to the Circle B ranch-house in the afternoon of the day following his men's visit to Horton's homestead. He banged on the door, and when Ballard opened it he went inside, and the two men walked through to the living-room. Ballard sat down, but Marlin paced up and down the room for a short while, the anger which was biting deep inside him, showing on his face. He stopped, and turned to face Ballard.

"Drummond and Morgan have vanished," he said, "just like Hill. When they left here late yesterday, they were heading for the Horton homestead, to persuade him to tell them where Kilcane and his friend are hiding out. The story in town is that Horton was found beaten up and dead outside his house last night, and they're burying him today. Seems nobody knows who the killers were. I'd say it's pretty certain that Drummond and Morgan were the ones, but where in tarnation have they got to? I told them to come straight back here, after they'd seen Horton."

"I can't help thinking," said Ballard, "that for an outfit I hired to get rid of the settlers for me, you ain't doing too good a job. That reputation of yours is liable to get a bit of a hammering if this gets out, don't you reckon?"

As he finished speaking he looked up into Marlin's face, then shrank back at the look of concentrated fury in the man's eyes.

"Just watch what you're saying, Ballard," said Marlin. "We hired on to get the settlers out, and that's what I aim to do. But first, I've got to find my men. I'm sure now that Kilcane and his friend are holding them somewhere. Just how they let themselves be taken, I can't understand. I'm going to comb every inch of this range for them. We've been working together for a long time."

"All right," said Ballard. "We'll leave the homesteaders alone for the time being. I've got two windmills I've got to get working again as soon as I can. Those men I sent after the rustlers have come back without finding any more trace of them, so I can let you have a few men, if you like."

"I don't want any help," said Marlin. "I reckon I stand a better chance of finding that hide-out on my own. I've done a bit of tracking in my time. If I need any help when I've located it, I'll come back here."

★ ★ ★

At the hide-out, Dan, Mary and Jack were discussing their next move.

"I reckon we've done pretty good to put three of the Liquidators out of action," said Dan. "Marlin must be hopping mad. He sure ain't used to being treated like this, and he'll be set on finding out where his men are, and on taking care of us personally. I figure he might come after us alone. It probably goes against the grain for Marlin to ask for help from anybody. It's usually the other way round.

"I ain't too keen," Dan continued, "on just hanging around, hoping he don't find us. I figure we should get him out here, to join his friends."

"How are we going to do that?" asked Jack.

"We'll keep a watch for him," replied Dan. "We'll take turns watching from the top of that high hill to the north there."

He pointed to a high, flat-topped hill, with gently sloping sides.

"We'll be able to see right down to the Circle B range from there," he went on. "Marlin's bound to ride this way, sooner or later. And that big black horse of his'll make him easy to spot. We'll figure out some way of getting him to the hide-out,

172

without him knowing he's been spotted by us."

For a while they discussed possible ways of luring Marlin to the hideout, then Dan and Jack went to drop some food to the prisoners. When they appeared at the pit entrance, the three men clustered underneath glared up at them.

"You've got a nerve, Kilcane, damn you," shouted Drummond. "Keeping us here, like this. You're dead men when Marlin catches up with you. And I reckon it won't be long before that happens."

"I'm counting on it," said Dan. "I reckon that pretty soon he'll be dropping in there to see you."

Drummond looked up at Dan, uncertainly, then took hold of the sack of food which Jack had lowered on a rope, and removed its contents.

"How long are you keeping us here?" shouted Morgan,

"That's hard to say," replied Dan. "It all depends on how long it takes to get a lawman here, to arrest you and Drummond for the murder of Horton."

A burst of profanity came from Drummond, as Jack pulled up the empty sack and he and Dan walked away from the pit entrance.

It was two days later when Jack, lying on top of the hill that they had selected as a look-out point from which to await Marlin's arrival, saw, early in the day, a lone rider on a big black horse.

The rider was heading slowly north, along the east boundary of the Circle B range, veering where necessary, to inspect any areas which might contain a possible hiding place.

Jack waited until he was sure that the approaching rider was Marlin, and that there were no other riders in sight. Then he climbed a short way down the side of the hill remote from the rider and, facing the sun, he took a mirror from his pocket and flashed a signal towards the hollow where Mary and Dan were watching. Mary saw it first, and called out to Dan.

Quickly, Dan ran over to a large prepared pile of brushwood and grass in the middle of the hollow, and lit it. It was soon sending a column of smoke up into the air. Seeing this, Jack resumed his previous position, and continued to watch the rider. He saw Marlin suddenly stop his mount, look towards the smoke, then head in that direction.

Jack moved to the position from which he had signalled earlier, and sent another pre-arranged signal to let Dan know that Marlin was heading towards the smoke. Then he climbed to the top of the hill again, and watched the rider's progress, as he rode cautiously towards the smoke, clearing by several hundred yards the foot of the hill from which Jack was observing him.

When he thought it safe to do so, Jack climbed down the hill, went for his mount, which he had hidden nearby, and followed Marlin. He could see that the smoke was now dying down. As

Marlin got closer to the source of the smoke, Jack saw that he was moving more cautiously, and as Jack watched from the cover of a large boulder, he saw the man he was following dismount and tie his horse behind a large rock outcrop. Then he saw Marlin proceed on foot, and lie down near the rim of the hollow in which the cabin was located.

Looking down into the hollow, Marlin could see the smoke still rising from the dying embers of the fire which Dan had started. Then, as his eyes started to search the hollow, he saw two people, a man and a woman, standing near a patch of brush on one side of the basin. From the descriptions he had been given, he was sure that they were Dan Kilcane and Ballard's stepdaughter, Mary.

Marlin felt uneasy. He wondered what the purpose of the fire had been, and where McLaren was. He carefully scrutinized every part of the hollow, but could see no sign of Dan's partner. He decided to ride back to the Circle B for reinforcements. But he was too late. Suddenly, the muzzle of a Peacemaker .45 was thrust hard into the back of his neck, and his six-gun was removed from its holster. He froze, and made no move until Jack ordered him to stand up, and start walking down into the hollow.

Marlin said nothing as he rose, but there was murder in his eyes as he turned to look at Jack, and the Peacemaker in his hand.

Jack's face was bleak. "Get moving," he ordered. Marlin hesitated for a moment, then started to walk down the slope.

Dan saw them coming, and he and Mary immediately started to scatter the remaining material on the fire, and stamp out the flames on the burning parts. By the time Jack had reached them with his prisoner, the smoke had almost completely died down.

"Well, Marlin," said Dan. "It's clear this assignment ain't going too well for you. Maybe you and your men are getting past it."

Observing Marlin closely, Dan saw the flare of intense anger in the man's eyes. He continued:

"I know that you and your gang have killed a lot of men, Marlin," he said, "and those men were generally prodded into drawing a gun on you, so's you could claim self-defence. But you and I know, Marlin, that what really happened was just plain murder, taking into account that you and your gang are all professional gunfighters.

"But it's different this time, Marlin," Dan went on. "Horton had no gun when he was murdered by Morgan and Drummond. And Horton's wife witnessed the killing. You're finished, Marlin. I'm going to see to it, personally, that the law takes care of you."

Marlin sneered. "We're a long way from the law here," he said. "Where are my men?"

"We're taking you to meet them

right now," replied Dan. "I guess it's going to be a touching reunion for all of you."

They took Marlin over to the mouth of the pit, and lowered him into it, as they had done with the others. His arrival was greeted by a volley of curses from the inmates, as they realized that any hopes of a rescue by their leader had now vanished.

Leaving the pit entrance, Jack headed for the lookout point, and Dan and Mary walked towards the cabin.

"Mary," said Dan, suddenly. "I'm getting kind of used to having you around, and I don't like the idea of us splitting up when this is all over. D'you figure that maybe you could settle down one day with a drifter like me, if I could find something worthwhile to do, in a place that suited the two of us?"

She looked across at him, and studied his face for a moment. Then she smiled.

"I've got to admit," she said, "that

you've growed on me as well. And life's been so hectic since we first met, that I'd be bound to miss you if we parted company. I'm pretty sure that we could make a go of it. I'm taking it that it's marriage that you have in mind?"

"Nothing less," smiled Dan, putting his arm around her shoulders, as they walked towards the cabin. Looking back at them as he climbed out of the hollow, Jack smiled to himself.

Dan decided, later in the day, that he had better pay Rennie a visit after dark, to find out if Ballard had been giving the homesteaders any more trouble, and to collect the provisions Rennie was holding for him. Mary persuaded him to let her go along.

They set off at dusk, leaving Jack in charge of the prisoners, and reached the Rennie homestead without incident. They dismounted at the barn, and leaving their horses there, walked towards the house, then stopped. Dan called out his name several times, and after a brief conversation with Rennie through the closed door, the homesteader let them in. They sat down in the living-room with Rennie, whose wife was in bed.

Rennie told them that Horton's wife had insisted on going back to her homestead, and that there had been no trouble from Ballard's men since Horton had been killed. Dan, feeling that Rennie was a man he could trust, told him that Marlin and his men were imprisoned at the hide-out. He also decided to tell him where the hide-out was located, in case the homesteader wanted to contact him in an emergency. This he did, asking Rennie to keep the information strictly to himself. Then he handed some money over, and asked Rennie to buy some more provisions for them, which they would collect in a few days' time.

Soon afterwards, Dan and Mary set off for the hideout, Dan carrying the supplies that Rennie had been holding for them. They were approaching the point where they intended to turn off the track, in order to cross the Circle B boundary, and climb out of the valley, when Dan stopped his horse as they were passing a small grove of trees on their right. Mary followed suit.

"Thought I heard something, Mary," said Dan. "How about you?"

"I heard nothing," she said.

But Dan had been right. As they started forward again, two rifles opened fire on them from the grove. Mary's horse was hit, and it went down, Mary falling with it. Dan was dazed by a bullet which gouged a furrow along the side of his head. He fell forward, then grabbed the pommel as his horse bolted. Somehow, he stayed in the saddle, but he had no idea how far the horse had gone before it came to a standstill. Then he lost consciousness, and fell sideways out of the saddle to the ground.

When he came to, his horse was standing close by, still carrying the sack of provisions. He took his watch out, struck a match and looked at the time. He estimated that it was about an hour since they had been ambushed. Looking to the east, he could see, silhouetted against the night sky, the high ground bordering the valley, and from the familiar shape of this silhouette, he was able to estimate his position. He reckoned he was about two mile south of the place where he and Mary had been fired on. Thinking back, he could remember seeing Mary go down with her horse, and he was hopeful that she had not been hit herself.

His head was aching violently. Gingerly, he put his hand up to the side of his head, and felt the wound. There seemed to be a little congealed blood along it, but the bleeding now appeared to have stopped.

He mounted, and headed back for the place where he had been shot. About four hundred yards from the grove, he tied his horse to a small tree, and proceeded cautiously on foot. When he reached the grove, there was no sign of Mary, nor of the men who had ambushed them. Dan was sure that they must have been Ballard's men, and that they would have taken Mary to the Circle B. They must, he thought, have been lying in wait at that particular point on the track, just on the off chance that he or Jack would be using it at night. He decided to ride back to the hide-out, to let Jack know what had happened, and to work out a plan to rescue Mary.

As he approached the hide-out, he gave a pre-arranged signal to Jack, on lookout, and rode up to him. Dawn was not far away. He explained briefly what had happened, and the two men went to the cabin, where Jack had a look at the wound on his partner's head, bathed it, and put a bandage on it.

"A nasty graze," he said. "You feel all right?"

"A bad headache, is all," replied Dan. "It'll soon go. What I'm more bothered about, is what are we going to do about Mary? I don't suppose Ballard will harm her. But we know how she feels about him. She won't stay with him willingly. I've got to get her away from there, and I'll need your help. We'll ride over there tonight, after dark. It's not going to be easy, because Ballard may be expecting a visit from us."

"We'll have to leave Marlin and the others here alone, then?" said Jack.

"We ain't got no option," said Dan. "But they can't climb out of that pit on their own. And anyway, they won't know we're missing, so long as we look in on them late afternoon, like we usually do. As soon as we've freed Mary, we'll hightail it back here."

"Right," said Jack. "Looks like tonight's going to be a busy one. We'd better get some rest."

10

THEY set off around sunset, after Jack had scanned the surrounding terrain to make sure it was clear of riders. They took a third horse with them, for Mary. On their way to the ranch buildings, they rode as far as possible across the open range, avoiding any places where Ballard might have stationed ambushers, under cover, to challenge night riders.

They reached the ranch buildings soon after midnight, and stopped at the pasture fence, well away from the house. The sky was overcast, and the buildings and the tall windmill which Jack had noticed on his earlier visit, showed up only as outlines against the night sky. No lights were showing in the buildings. They dismounted, and tied the three horses to the fence.

"Jack," said Dan, "will you scout around, and see if Ballard has posted any guards. And see if you can see a door or a window at the back of the ranch-house. I'll wait here for you."

"Sure," said Jack, and melted into the darkness. He returned twenty minutes later.

"No guards outside," he reported, "and nobody in the barn. And if anybody happened to be watching from inside any of the other buildings, I made sure they didn't see me.

"There's one window at the back of the ranchhouse," he went on, "but no door. It's only a little window, but big enough to climb through. Maybe it's a storeroom."

"Right," said Jack. "Now I figure Ballard wants us two pretty bad. He's not a fool, and he'll guess that we'll be set on taking Mary away from here. I figure that he's got men inside the ranch-house waiting to take us, when we go in there after Mary. The way he sees it, it'll be a lot easier to catch us that way."

"I think you're right," said Jack, "and just to make sure, he's probably got more than just a couple of men inside."

"Yes," agreed Dan. "And that means we've got to get them out of the house somehow, before we can get to Mary. Was there any hay in the barn, Jack?"

"Yes," replied Jack. "I ran into a big pile of it when I walked inside."

"Right," said Jack. "This is what we do, then." He went on to describe a plan of action to Jack.

When he had finished, they left the three horses tied to the pasture fence, and walked over to the barn. Then, screened by the barn and the bunkhouse from anyone who might be watching from the ranch-house, they carried a number of armfuls of loose, dry hay from the barn, and piled it around and between the four stout timber supporting legs of the windmill tower.

When Dan judged that they had placed enough hay in position, he struck several matches, throwing them on to the hay, at different points, while Jack went to the barn, and threw a lighted match on to the remaining hay inside. Then they ran together, skirting the bunkhouse and the ranch-house at a distance, and approached the ranch-house from the rear. They stood against the wall, close to the window, which was near to the corner of the house.

All was quiet for a while. Then, as Dan peered round the corner of the building, and saw the glow from the burning hay, a sudden hullabaloo arose inside the ranch-house. Dan took from his pocket, a rusty old chisel he had found in the cabin, and under cover of the noise, he forced the window open. They could hear Ballard's voice inside.

"You, Smith, and you, Farley," he was shouting. "Stay there upstairs, and guard that bedroom door. The rest of you, come with me. Except you,

Durham. Stand inside the door here, and shoot any stranger who tries to come in from outside."

Dan and Jack heard several men run out of the house, then they heard the sound of their voices, as they ran towards the fires. Dan knew that Ballard would be desperately anxious to save both the windmill and the barn.

Dan climbed through the window he had just opened, and Jack squeezed through behind him. They found themselves in what appeared to be a small storeroom, whose door was very slightly ajar. Jack pushed the door open a little further, and saw that it opened into the living-room. He could see the figure of a man, outlined by the light from the flames, standing in the doorway leading to the outside. His back was towards them.

Dan opened the door wide, and he and Jack walked up behind the man, Durham, in the doorway. Jack locked an arm around the man's throat, while Dan relieved him of his gun. Jack tightened his hold around the man's throat, then released it slightly, as he saw that his victim was beginning to lose consciousness.

Dan held his face close to Durham's, and spoke to him.

"Call your friends Smith and Farley down from upstairs," he said. "Tell them Ballard wants them to help with the fires. Say you're staying on guard down here."

Durham shook his head. Dan nodded to his partner, and Jack tightened his arm around Durham's throat again, until his victim frantically tried to nod his head, as his face was slowly turning purple. Jack released his hold a little, and pulled Durham nearer to the bottom of the stairs, but out of sight of the landing at the top.

"Start talking," said Dan, softly.

Durham had to clear his throat before he could speak clearly.

"Smith," he shouted, "Mr Ballard wants you and Farley to go and help with the fires. I'm staying on guard down here."

As Smith shouted that he was coming, Jack released his hold on Durham, and Dan hit the ranch-hand on the head with the barrel of his Peacemaker. Durham slumped to the floor. Smith and Farley, coming down the stairs immediately after, were unexpectedly confronted by Jack and his partner, and both suffered the same fate as Durham.

"Watch these three, Jack," said Dan, and ran quickly upstairs. He found two bedroom doors, one of them locked on the outside. He opened this one, and walked inside. He could see Mary at the window, looking out at the fires, which were still burning fiercely. She turned as he walked towards her.

"It's Dan," he said, and she ran up to him. He took her in his arms for a few moments, then spoke again.

"Get dressed, Mary," he said. "We've got to move fast, and get out of here before Ballard comes back in."

While Mary hurriedly dressed, by the light from the fires, Dan tore two of the bed sheets into strips. Then they went downstairs, and Dan and Jack quickly bound and gagged the three ranch-hands, who were showing signs of coming round. Then all three climbed out of the rear window of the house, and giving the fires a wide berth, they headed for the horses waiting at the pasture fence, mounted them, and rode off.

★ ★ ★

East of the hide-out, half an hour after Dan and Jack had left, Ben Bridger, a lone prospector, rode his mule out of a long stretch of broken ground, and headed in the direction of the hollow in which the hidden cabin was located. Behind the mule trailed a loaded burro.

Bridger was a slim, short, elderly man, slightly bent, bearded, and wearing a battered old hat, with clothing to suit.

He paused on the rim of the hollow, and looked down into it. Then, judging it to be a good place to spend the night, he turned the mule, and urged it down the slope. When he reached the bottom of the hollow, he rode along it, looking for a suitable place to camp. He dismounted ten yards short of the pit entrance, and looked around. Seeing what appeared to be a hole in the ground, he walked over, and looked in to it.

Startled at what he saw, he immediately stepped back. He was sure he had seen a light well down below the level of the ground he was standing on. He listened intently, and heard the faint sounds of voices from below. They were not loud enough for him to distinguish what was being said.

He stood for a while, unsure as to what to do next. He knew he could easily draw the attention of the people in the pit to himself, but he wasn't sure that would be a wise move. He decided to scout round, in the failing light, to see if there was another entrance to the pit anywhere nearby. He found none, but during his search, he came upon the cabin, and the horses tethered behind it. The cabin was obviously being used. He lit a lamp which he found inside it.

Bridger was at a loss to understand the presence of the men underground, with no apparent means of exit from the pit. He was an inquisitive man, and it wasn't long before his curiosity got the better of him, and any apprehension he might have felt took a back seat. He walked over to the hole, and leant forward a little, to look down into it.

"You down there," he shouted.

The conversation below ceased abruptly, and a moment later Marlin and his men appeared underneath the hole, within Bridger's range of vision. One of them was carrying an oil lamp, which he placed on the floor.

"Who're you?" called Marlin.

"Name's Bridger," said the old man. "I've just arrived in these parts, to do a bit of prospecting, and heard you men talking. What in tarnation are you doing down there?"

"We've been expecting some friends to turn up in the hollow there," said Marlin. "You seen any sign of them?"

"No," replied Bridger. "I found a cabin in the brush, but it's empty, and there's nobody up here but myself."

"You asked what we're doing down here," said Marlin. "I've got to tell you we feel mighty foolish, because we all climbed down into this pit with a lamp, to have a look around, and just when the last one was climbing down, darned if the rope we'd tied around that boulder up there didn't come loose, and fall down inside here."

"That's all right," said Bridger. "Just throw it up here, and I'll fix it for you again."

"Can't do that," said Marlin. "The darned rope fell in the stream that's running through here, and got washed away before we could stop it."

"Where are you from?" asked Bridger.

"We work on the Circle B ranch just west of here," replied Marlin. "We sure are glad you happened along. You got a rope with you?"

"Yes," replied Bridger.

"Well," said Marlin. "If you knot it, and tie it around that boulder up there, we'd like you to come down here, and look around the wall of this pit. We think there are traces of gold down here, but we don't know enough about it to be sure. We need an expert's opinion."

Bridger's eyes gleamed. Maybe, he thought, his luck was going to change at last. Hurriedly, he took a length of rope from the burro, knotted it, tied it round the boulder, and dropped the free end through the hole in the ground. Then, slowly, he lowered himself into the pit.

As he reached the floor below, Drummond punched him hard on the side of the jaw, and the old man collapsed, unconscious. Marlin climbed out of the pit, followed closely by the other three. Drummond, the last one up, pulled the rope out of the pit, just as Bridger started to stir. He did not untie the rope from the boulder.

Marlin took Bridger's rifle from the burro, and the four men spread out, making sure there was no one in the hollow and its vicinity but themselves and Bridger. They all returned to the pit entrance, except Hill, who stayed on lookout. Bridger was now standing below the hole, shouting despairingly for a rope. He was scared that he was going to be left to a slow death from starvation.

Marlin and the others looked down at Bridger. "What do we do with him?" asked Drummond.

"He's in the way," said Marlin, "Kilcane and his partner could turn up at any minute. We can't let anything warn them that we're here. We'll have to finish him off.

"But we can't risk the sound of a shot," he went on. "Climb down there, Morgan, and do what's necessary.

Leave him down there, out of sight. And leave the lamp burning."

Morgan threw the end of the rope down and climbed down into the pit before Bridger could start to ascend. A moment later, a brief scream, quickly tailing off into silence, was heard from inside the pit, and shortly after, a bloodstained knife flew up out of the pit, and landed on the ground outside. Morgan climbed up the rope, retrieved the knife, and wiped it clean on a tuft of grass.

"What do we do now?" Drummond asked, as he untied the rope from the boulder.

"We stay here," replied Marlin. "One thing's certain. Kilcane and his partner will be coming back here. We'll have a surprise ready for them when they turn up."

The three men walked to the cabin, Drummond leading the mule and burro, which he tethered behind the building near the horses, before rejoining the others.

"We don't know when Kilcane and his friend will be turning up," said Marlin, "but it could be any time. See if there are any weapons in the cabin."

Marlin cursed when a careful search of the cabin revealed no hand-guns or rifles. This meant that he and his men had only one rifle between them, the one belonging to Bridger.

Marlin turned to Morgan.

"Bring Hill here, and we'll all wait in that thick brush near the side of the cabin," said Marlin. "When they get here, I'll step out, and hold the rifle on them, then you can get their guns. I can't wait to get my hands on them two."

"It's the same with the rest of us," said Drummond. "They sure made fools out of us. We've got to make them pay for that."

"They'll pay, all right," said Marlin. There was a baleful look in his eye, which boded ill for Dan and his partner.

11

ON their ride back to the hide-out, Dan and Jack, riding with Mary between them, made only slow progress in the dark, and dawn was not far away when they reached a point about half a mile from the hollow, close to a scattering of large boulders. Jack stopped, and the others followed suit.

"I'm near certain," said Jack, "that we ain't been followed, but I figure I'll hide in these rocks for a while, and watch the back trail, just to make absolutely sure."

"All right," said Dan. "See you later, then."

He rode on with Mary, towards the hollow.

"Did Ballard harm you at all?" he asked her.

"No," she replied. "He kept on at

201

me all the time to tell him where you and Jack were hiding out, but he didn't use any physical force against me. But he kept me locked in that bedroom all the time. He said he wouldn't let me out till I told him what he wanted to know. He's changed, really changed, since mother married him. All he seems to be interested in now, is making money, regardless of the rights of other people, and he sees you two as standing in his way."

They rode down into the hollow, and up to the entrance to the pit, where they dismounted. Dan looked down into the pit, and could see the dim light from the lamp, which the men down there usually kept lit during the night. Leading the horses, he and Mary walked into the brush, and towards the cabin. The light was growing stronger.

Suddenly, without warning, Marlin stepped out of the brush on their right, and held a rifle on them. His three men followed him. Seeing that these three were unarmed, Dan had a strong impulse to fight it out with Marlin. Sensing this, Marlin sent a bullet past Dan's ear.

"Don't be a fool, Kilcane," he said. "You wouldn't stand a chance. And who knows, the woman might get in the way of a bullet, as well."

Dan raised his hands, and was relieved of his gun by Drummond. Mary wasn't carrying a weapon.

"I'm disappointed, Kilcane," said Marlin "I was expecting McLaren to be with you. Maybe you'll tell me just where he is."

"We've split up," said Dan. "We figured we'd better hide in separate places, so we couldn't both be taken at the same time. But don't think I'm going to tell you where he is "

"I don't believe you, Kilcane," said Marlin. Then he spoke to Hill and Morgan.

"You two get horses from behind the cabin," he said, "and go and see if there's any sign of McLaren out there.

Take the rifles with you. I'll keep the six-gun. Come back here, when you've had a good look round."

Dan smiled to himself at the idea that Marlin's men could find Jack if he didn't want to be found.

The sun was rising as Hill and Morgan rode off, and Marlin told Dan and Mary to go into the cabin, where, with Marlin's rifle still pointing at them, their hands were tied by Drummond. They sat down on two chairs.

"I'm a mite curious," said Dan. "Just how did you manage to get out of that pit?"

"We had a great stroke of luck," replied Marlin. "A wandering prospector came along, and heard us talking down there. I managed to persuade him to drop a rope down to us."

"I can see he ain't around now," said Dan. "I suppose you had to kill him."

"It had to be done," said Marlin. "The fewer people who know about us being held prisoner here, the better. You must see that. We have our reputations to think of."

Mary turned her head away in disgust.

"*We* know about it," said Dan.

"More than that," said Marlin, "*you* were the cause of it, and that's why you're going to die, not because Ballard paid us to do the job. And the same goes for that partner of yours, when we get hold of him."

"And what about Miss Ballard here?" asked Dan.

"She'll be going back to the Circle B," replied Marlin. "It's up to Ballard to decide what's going to happen to her."

Shortly after this, Marlin and Drummond left the cabin for a while, leaving Dan and Mary with hands tied, and fastened to the chairs on which they were sitting.

"D'you think that the two who went after Jack will catch him?" asked Mary.

Dan shook his head. "Not a chance,"

he said. "When Jack heard that rifle shot, he'd know something was wrong here, and he'd be watching out for Marlin's men."

"What's going to happen to us?" asked Mary.

"I ain't worried too much," replied Dan, "not with Jack on the loose. If Marlin keeps us here overnight, we'd best stay awake, and ready for anything."

Shortly after, Marlin and Drummond came back into the cabin, and sat there until they heard Hill and Morgan returning, two hours later. Marlin went outside to meet them.

"Ain't no sign of McLaren anywhere around here," said Hill. "I figure Kilcane and the woman came alone. What do we do now?"

"We stay here overnight," replied Marlin, "and we keep up a two-man watch for McLaren all the time, day and night. We'll take it in turns. If McLaren doesn't turn up before morning, we'll take Kilcane and the woman to Ballard. I'm going to ask Ballard to hand Kilcane over to me, because after what he did to us, we don't want him to die quick. And the same goes for McLaren too."

The rest of the day passed without incident. At midnight, Hill and Drummond relieved Marlin and Morgan, and took up positions on opposite sides of the rim of the hollow, too far apart to be able to see one another in the dark. The night was still. They both found a large boulder to lean against, and settled back against it, relying on their ears to give them warning of anyone approaching the hollow.

It was almost an hour after they had started their vigil that a faint sound, a few feet in front of Drummond, broke the silence. He craned his head forward, but could see nothing. Then the sound, a little louder this time, was repeated, as Jack threw the second small stone, and moved up noiselessly behind Drummond who took a single step forward, and was starting to raise his rifle, when Jack clubbed him from behind with the barrel of his six-gun.

Drummond fell to the ground, and Jack quickly tied and gagged him, then dragged him up against the foot of the boulder. Then, moving silently from cover to cover, Jack worked his way around the rim of the hollow, and approached the boulder against which Hill was leaning. He had already located Hill's position, earlier on.

Hill's right shoulder was against the boulder, and Jack approached him from the rear, until he could clearly see the outline of the figure of his quarry. He paused, then prepared to provide a distraction, just as he had done with Drummond. But suddenly Hill turned to face Jack, warned not by any sound, but by a sudden instinct that he was in danger. He saw Jack's outline, and started to raise his rifle.

Unable to fire, because of the likelihood that the sound of the shot would alert Marlin, Jack quickly pulled his knife from its sheath, grasped the blade, and threw the weapon at the man in front of him. As the steel blade entered his heart, Hill dropped his rifle, staggered back a few steps, clutching ineffectually at the knife handle, then dropped, and lay still. Jack ran up to him, his six-gun in his hand, to find that his adversary was dead. He withdrew his knife from the wound, and wiped the blade clean.

Jack made his way down to the cabin, and stood outside it for a moment. A light was burning inside. He risked a brief look through the bottom of a window, and breathed a sigh of relief, as he saw Dan and Mary, seated on chairs against the far wall. He could also see Marlin, lying on the bed, and Morgan, lying on the floor close by. So far as he could tell, they were both asleep. With his six-gun in his hand, Jack quietly opened the cabin door, and entered.

Dan and Mary were both awake. Relief showed in their eyes as they saw him. Looking across at Marlin and Morgan, Jack saw the six-gun on the small table close to Marlin's bed. He tiptoed over, picked it up, and pushed it under his belt. As he did so, he could see that Marlin was beginning to stir. He sent a bullet into the wooden floor, halfway between the two men, followed by another, as they jerked into wakefulness. Then he ordered them to lay still. Keeping them covered, he walked over to Dan, and cut his hands free. Then he handed the knife to Dan, who freed himself from the chair, cut the rope around his ankles, and then freed Mary.

"Good to see you, Jack," said Dan. "Knew you'd be along sooner or later."

Jack told Dan about his encounters with Hill and Drummond, and when it was daylight they took Marlin and Morgan to the pit entrance, and Jack went to bring Drummond down to join them. Before they lowered the men down, Dan climbed down into the pit, and confirmed the suspicion he had that the old prospector's body was lying there. They hauled the body out, then lowered Marlin and his two men into the pit, as they had done on a previous occasion. The prisoners said nothing during these proceedings, but their complete sense of frustration and anger at once more being consigned to the pit, was clearly evident in their faces, as they looked murderously at Dan and his two companions.

Mary went back to the cabin, leaving Jack and Dan to bury the bodies of Hill and the prospector. Later, they joined her for a few hours' rest.

★ ★ ★

At the Circle B ranch-house, when Ballard got up that same morning, he was in an angry frame of mind, brought on by Mary's recent escape, and the considerable fire damage to the barn and the windmill. After breakfast, he walked across to the bunkhouse, to see if Marlin had returned during the night, but there was no sign of him.

He began to get the feeling that maybe Marlin had disappeared, just like his men. And all the time, his own plan for getting the settlers out of the valley was being held up, mainly, he was sure, by two men, Kilcane and his partner.

He called one of his men over, Cass Black by name. Black had been with him a long time. He was a burly man, in his early thirties, not averse to operating a little outside the law, if Ballard paid him accordingly.

"Cass," said Ballard, "I'm tired of waiting to get my hands on Kilcane and McLaren, and it's beginning to look like I wasted my money bringing Marlin and his men in to help out. I've got to find out where Kilcane and his partner are hiding out. Go into town, and stay there. Keep your eyes and ears open, and spend some time in the store, and the other places the homesteaders go into. Maybe it's a long shot, but I'm hoping that you might hear something that'll help us to find Kilcane's hide-out. I'm sure at least one of the homesteaders knows where it is."

Black set off for town twenty minutes later, and when he arrived there, he tied his horse outside the saloon, and went in for a drink. There were no homesteaders inside. Finishing his drink, he had a walk around town. There weren't any buckboards in sight, and there was no sign of settlers in any of the places of business. He was standing, undecided, outside the restaurant, when he saw two buckboards coming into town. As they drew nearer, he saw that the first one was carrying Rennie and his wife, and the second one was being driven by Frost, with his wife and daughter by his side.

The buckboards stopped outside the store, and the two families went inside. After a couple of minutes, Black followed them, and pretended to be examining some items at the back of the store, while Sam Blair and his wife were attending to the homesteaders. Black listened intently to the conversation.

Blair, who was serving the Rennies, started stacking the provisions on their list on to the counter. Before he had finished, the Frosts had loaded their provisions on to their buckboard, and were ready to leave. Blair placed the last item on the Rennie's list on to the counter. He spoke jokingly to the Rennies, gesturing at the big pile in front of him.

"You folks sure have developed healthy appetites lately," he said. "Must be all that hard work you're doing on the homestead. But I ain't complaining. It's sure good for business."

Rennie smiled, and quickly changed the subject. Black stayed in the store until Rennie left. Then, thoughtfully, he looked after the homesteaders as they left town. He decided it was time for a talk with Ballard.

When Black reached the ranch-house, he found Ballard inside. He told the rancher about Blair's comments on the size of Rennie's purchase of provisions.

"Good work, Cass!" exclaimed Ballard. "I'd say it's pretty clear that Rennie's buying provisions for Kilcane and the others. Kilcane stayed with him for a while. So it's likely that Rennie knows where Kilcane's hiding out. Tell Boyle to come and see me right away."

When the foreman came in, a few minutes later, Ballard told him what Black had heard in the store.

"We've got to make Rennie talk," he went on. "It's time to stop playing around. Take eight men, and rush his place after dark. Don't let him get any shots off to warn the neighbours. And when you've got hold of him, find out where Kilcane is. Do whatever you have to do, to get it out of him. And when you've done that, hightail it back here. I'll have another seven men waiting for you here, to go with you after Kilcane and his friend. This time, with a bit of luck, we'll get them."

At the Rennie homestead, half an hour after darkness had fallen, and while the homesteader and his wife were taking a meal, there was a sudden rattle from the tin cans on the alarm system, and Rennie started to rise. A moment later, three men carrying a heavy log, who had made a run at the door, battered it down, and entered. Before Rennie could reach his rifle, hanging on the wall, Ballard's foreman, Boyle, ran up to him, held a gun against his head, and ordered him to sit down on a chair. Then, roughly, he ordered Martha Rennie to sit on a chair on the other side of the room.

Boyle looked at Rennie for a moment. Then he walked to the door, and spoke to the five men outside.

"You men scatter," he said, "and watch out for anyone coming up to the house. If anybody does turn up, bring them inside."

He closed the door, and walked over to stand in front of Rennie. Grimly, he looked down at the homesteader.

Then he went over to a large sack standing against the wall, near the stove. Looking into it, he could see it was full of provisions. He walked back to Rennie.

"You can see this ain't a social call, Rennie," he said. "We're here for some information. We're sure you know where Kilcane and McLaren are hiding. Just tell us where that is, and we'll be on our way."

"Ballard must be crazy to send you here," said Rennie, heatedly. "Even if I knew, I wouldn't tell you. Kilcane and his partner have been good friends to us homesteaders."

Boyle's face hardened, and he told two of his men to tie Rennie and his wife firmly to the chairs on which they were sitting. Then he spoke to Rennie.

"I ain't had much experience in making people talk," he said, "but I don't think I'll waste any time beating you up, Rennie."

He walked over to Rennie's wife, and

looked down at her. Then he walked over to a table near the stove, and picked up a small sharp-pointed knife. He returned to Martha Rennie.

"This is a handsome woman you've got here, Rennie," said Boyle, "but she ain't going to look so good with a couple of knife slashes down her cheeks. And she ain't going to thank you for letting it happen to her."

"Damn you, Boyle!" shouted Rennie. Frantically, he tried to rise, but the two men standing by him held him down.

Boyle positioned the knife so that the point was just touching the woman's cheek. She cringed back against the chair.

"This is your last chance, Rennie," said Boyle.

"All right!" shouted Rennie, thinking fast. "All right! Leave her be."

"The hide-out, Rennie," said Boyle. "Where's the hide-out?"

"It's way on the far side of the Circle B range," replied Rennie, "about a mile outside the west boundary.

There's a couple of mesas about half a mile apart, that can be seen from miles away, and just west of these mesas, there's a box canyon. That's where the hide-out is. In a big cave in the canyon wall."

"I know the canyon you're talking about," said Boyle, "and I looked up it from the entrance once, but I didn't see no cave."

"There's some brush growing up against the wall," said Rennie. "The cave entrance is behind that."

"I remember seeing the brush," said Boyle to the other Circle B men in the room. "Looks like we've got what we came for."

He told one of the men to untie Mrs Rennie, then he spoke to the homesteader.

"We're leaving now, Rennie," he said. "If it turns out you've been lying about that hide-out, you can be sure we'll be back." He threw the knife down on the table, and left the house with the other men. Shortly after,

Rennie and his wife heard the sound of riders leaving. She went over to him, and untied the rope holding him to the chair.

"I'm sorry," she said, "that because of me, you had to tell Boyle where Mr Kilcane and his friend are. What's going to become of them?"

"Don't you fret none about that, Martha," he replied. "When they reach that box canyon I told them about, they won't find no cave, and they'll be about twenty five miles from where Kilcane and the others are *really* hiding out."

She stared at him, wide-eyed. "You lied!" she said.

"I sure did," he said, "and that's why we're leaving here, right now. You heard what Boyle said about coming back. We'll take a couple of horses, and ride over to Kilcane's hide-out. It's a fine, clear night. And we'd better take that sack of provisions with us."

12

IT was in the early hours, when Jack, at the lookout point on the rim of the hollow, heard the Rennies approaching. He heard Rennie repeatedly calling his own name, and he recognized the voice. He stepped out from behind his cover, and called to them. They stopped as they reached him, and Rennie told Jack what had happened.

"Better come down to the cabin," said Jack, and led the way. As they passed close to the pit, he pointed it out to them. They followed him into the cabin, where he lit the lamp, awakening Dan and Mary. Mary came out from behind her curtain, and she and Dan looked at the Rennies, surprised. Rennie repeated to them what he had already told Jack.

"That box canyon where I said you

were hiding out," he went on. "We spent a night there, when I was driving our covered wagon into the valley, to look for a homestead. It's a good thing I remembered it."

"We're mighty grateful you didn't put them on to us here," said Dan. "It was a brave thing you did. You'd better stay with us here.

"It's clear Ballard's got to be stopped," he went on. "We've got to get him into the pit with Marlin and the others, and keep him there."

After finding out from Rennie what time Boyle had left his homestead, Dan carried out a few quick calculations in his head.

"If Jack and I set off now, we could reach the Circle B ranch-house *after* Ballard's men have set out for that box canyon, and well before they get back and tell him he's been fooled. He's so keen on catching us, that I guess he'll send most of his men to the canyon. But will he go himself? What d'you think, Mary?"

"There's no doubt in my mind," replied Mary. "He'll send his foreman with the hands, and he'll stay behind. He's never been one for riding at the head of his men, and I know he hates riding in the dark."

"Right," said Dan. "Then Jack and I have a good chance of bringing him back here. We'll leave right away.

"But before we go," he went on, "I figure the way this is boiling up, we've got to do something to try to get the law in on it. When I was in Fort Laramie, not long ago, I heard that a U.S. Marshal was due to be stationed there. He should be there by now. He's an ex-Army lieutenant called Farren, and a good friend of mine. I'm going to write him a letter right now, about the situation here, and I'll ask him to come here with some deputies."

He looked at Rennie.

"Would you ride to Fort Laramie, and hand that letter over to Farren?" he asked.

"Be glad to," replied Rennie. "When do I leave?"

"Right away," replied Dan. "Ride south-east from here, and you won't have to cross Circle B range."

Dan, Jack and the homesteader all left shortly after. Dan had a few words with Mary before he rode off.

"It won't be long before we're back here with Ballard," he said, "and maybe it won't be long after that before we can think of ourselves, for a change."

"I hope so. Look after yourself," she said, and watched him, as he and Jack gradually faded into the darkness.

It was around three in the morning when Dan and Jack approached the Circle B ranch buildings, and tied their horses to the pasture fence. The only light showing was in the ranch-house. Dan and Jack, circling the buildings, could find no evidence that guards had been posted. Warily, they approached the house, risked a look through a living-room window, and saw Ballard sitting at a table with two other men, playing cards. Dan guessed that he was whiling the time away, until he learnt whether Dan and Jack had been captured.

They walked round to the back of the house, and looked at the window which Dan had forced on their previous visit. It was held closed only by a thin wooden wedge, which fell out as Dan pulled the window towards him. They climbed through into the storeroom, opened the door into the living-room a fraction, and looked through the gap. The three men were still seated at the table.

"You ready?" whispered Dan. Jack nodded.

They drew their guns, then Dan pushed the door wide open, and they walked into the room. The man facing them half-rose, and started to go for his gun, but Jack sent a bullet which passed very close to the man's ear, and embedded itself in the wall. The man sat down very quickly, and raised his hands. Ballard and the other man remained motionless.

"Just keep your hands clear of those guns," ordered Dan. Then he and Jack walked up to two of the men, and relieved them of their guns. Ballard was unarmed. The rancher's face was a study as he saw who the intruders were. After tying the hands of the three men, Jack went to look inside the other buildings. He returned, to tell Jack that there were no more hands around.

"We're going for a ride," said Dan to Ballard. "We're taking you and your men to stay with Marlin and his partners."

"You won't get away with this, Kilcane," said Ballard. "There'll be sixteen men out looking for me soon."

"We'll be well away from here before they get back," said Dan. "We're leaving now. You'd better come quiet. If you don't, we'll lie you across the backs of your horses, and tie you on."

Jack brought three horses from the

pasture for the prisoners, and saddled them. Then he went into the cookhouse, and threw some provisions into a sack, ready to take with him, to help feed the mounting tally of prisoners in the pit. It was after daylight when they reached the hide-out, having encountered no one on the way. Mary and Martha Rennie were waiting for them on the rim of the hollow, and they followed the riders down to the pit.

After shouting to Marlin and his men to stand back, Jack and Dan lowered Ballard and his two hands into the pit, one by one, and deposited them on the floor. As they started to walk towards the cabin, they heard the voices of Ballard and Marlin raised in heated recriminations.

In the cabin, Dan told the two women what had happened at the ranch.

"What do we do now?" asked Mary, when he had finished.

"We sit tight here," replied Dan, "and wait for John to get back. And meantime, we keep a sharp lookout, and hope that Boyle doesn't find us."

When the Circle B foreman, Boyle, got back to the ranch-house, after a fruitless mission, and found that Ballard and his two men were missing, he could only guess at what might have happened.

He sent a hand into town to enquire whether anyone had seen the rancher there. No one had. When Ballard hadn't shown up by evening, Boyle decided that Dan and Jack must be holding him, with Marlin and his men. He decided to start out on a systematic search for the rancher on the following morning. He felt sure now, that the hide-out was not on Circle B range. That had already been carefully swept. He decided to search an area outside the whole length of the boundary, and adjacent to it.

The search would be carried out thoroughly and methodically, by himself and fifteen hands, and they would take a buckboard with them, carrying provisions. They would start their search at a point due south of the ranch-house, moving along outside the boundary in a westerly direction.

At the hide-out, Dan, Jack and the two women awaited the return of Rennie and the law officers, in what they hoped would be about three days' time.

"Up to now," said Dan, "we've been lucky that nobody's spotted this hide-out. But I've got a feeling our luck ain't going to last much longer. While you ladies watch out for Circle B riders coming our way, we'll build ourselves a place where we can shelter from fire, and stop anybody from coming down here."

He and Jack proceeded to build a circular wall, its diameter being sufficient to allow four people to crouch inside it, and high enough to shield them against rifle fire from the rim of the hollow. They used the loose stones which were liberally scattered over the ground close by. When it was finished, they put water, food and ammunition inside.

Three days later, in the afternoon, Jack, on watch at the rim of the hollow, saw the line of Circle B men approaching from the north. He could see that there was no chance of them missing the hollow, and he was sure that at least one of them would decide to ride down into it. He ran to warn the others, then all four of them climbed inside the circular wall, carrying their rifles with them. Jack and Dan were both expert riflemen. The women, although knowing how to use the weapon, were not so deadly. They all crouched down, watching through small gaps in the stones at the top of the wall.

Suddenly two riders appeared on the north rim of the hollow, paused for a moment, then started to ride down the slope into it. Jack shot one, Dan the other. Both fell out of their saddles, and lay still. For a while, there were no signs of movement, then two men

230

crawled on their bellies up to the rim, and looked down at the two men lying motionless on the slope. They both cursed as two rifle bullets hit the slope just underneath their faces, and both crawled hurriedly backwards, out of sight.

At first, there was no shooting from the fourteen Circle B men who had assembled at the top of the hollow at the sound of the shooting, but Jack and Dan caught fleeting glimpses of them as they moved around the rim of the hollow to surround it, and took what cover they could find. A hail of rifle bullets rattled against the stone wall. Then there was silence.

"They've lost two men," said Dan, "so I figure they're going to wait for an hour or so, until it's dark. And when it is, they're going to come down here, and rush us. And I figure they've got us well outnumbered. Best thing is to stay here, and shoot as many as we can, as soon as we can see them. I don't think it's going to be all that dark tonight. You ladies wait till you're sure of hitting your target before you fire."

Standing next to Dan, as the sun slowly dipped towards the horizon, Mary slipped her hand in his, as all four of them peered through the top of the wall, watching for any move on the part of the Circle B men.

Then, suddenly, they heard shots, not directed at them, and saw a troop of U.S. Cavalry, on the charge, circling the rim of the hollow, then slowing down to flush out the Circle B men from their cover. It was not long before the shooting died down, and they saw three men riding down into the hollow towards them. Martha Rennie cried out with relief, as she recognized one as her husband. The others were an Army lieutenant, and a tall man wearing a U.S. Marshal's badge.

"Howdy, Dan," said U.S. Marshal Farren. "Glad we got here in time. I didn't have no deputies free, so I persuaded the Army to lend a hand. This is Lieutenant Bodean. His men are holding the Circle B men prisoner up above. They didn't have any stomach for a fight with the Cavalry."

When the introductions were over, Farren continued: "Mr Rennie was telling us about that place where you're holding Marlin and his men," he said. "We'd sure like to see it."

"We've got Ballard in there as well now, with two of his men," said Dan, as they walked over to the mouth of the pit and looked down into it. The six occupants, curious about the gunfire, were staring up at them. Marlin's face purpled with rage, as he recognized Dan and Jack, and saw a U.S. Marshal, and an officer in Army uniform beside them.

Looking at Farren, Dan saw the grim smile on his face.

"What a comedown for Marlin," said the marshal. "He sure can't be used to this kind of treatment. Nor Ballard too, for that matter."

The following day the troop set off for Fort Laramie with the prisoners. Farren accompanied them. At the subsequent trial, Marlin and his men, together with Ballard, were all sentenced to death by hanging.

Shortly after this, County Sheriff Brand was removed from office, and Dan was offered the job, and accepted. He built a small house on the outskirts of town, and settled down there with Mary.

And so it was that peace finally descended on the valley.

THE END